BUNDLE IN THE MACHINE AND OTHER TALL STORIES

Simon J Ellis

Also by Simon J Ellis

THE LEA BRIDGE ROAD SHANTYMEN
FRANCIS TROCKLEY REGGAEMAN
THE BEAUFORT STIPENDIARY

BUNDLE IN THE MACHINE AND OTHER TALL STORIES

Simon J Ellis

PREFACE TO THE FIRST EDITION

I have called this a collection of tall stories, partly to give it character but mainly to indicate the level of veracity to the reader.

When we hear someone telling tall stories, our suspicions are rightly aroused, as they should also be here. But in order to hoodwink the reader, I, like every other dissembler, have buried some truth in my narrative.

The reader may, therefore, be assured that I have carried out my side of the bargain in every one of these tales. Sometimes, I have made it obvious, but beware! What may appear to be the most outrageous claim on willingness to suspend disbelief may actually approximate or even reproduce fact.

July 2020

Contents (not applicable to e-book)

1. BUNDLE IN THE MACHINE

'So, I said to Piggy, I said, "I'm gonna have to run home". He said, "Why?" I said, "Because of the missus". And he said, "But Norman, you're not married". And I said... "No. I'm talking about my darts playing!"

'See how drink gets to everything? Even place names have meanings. Azerbaijan means, "Can you order me a taxi?"

'But seriously folks, it's wonderful to see so many of you here tonight, especially the youngsters. So here's my big thank you to everyone who took part: the dancers, the singers, the magicians, and, of course, our beloved comedians. This is how Piggy would have wanted it.

'We have raised over five thousand pounds! Yes... yes... and I know how grateful Jenny and the kids are. So let's finish by singing Piggy's favourite song, as we always do.'

The applause that had intercepted every pause till the end of the speech became frantic. Lights criss-crossed over the audience whilst a dance troupe jigged their way from the wings to the front of the stage to join the other entertainers. As the cheering grew louder, the orchestra struck up the fanfare opening to "I'm Always Smiling". Norman began to sing the first verse, but his hot tears became uncontrollable, so he waved his arms in the fashion of a mad conductor to encourage the audience to take over during the chorus. They did so as a body, along with the colourfully dressed entertainers, and he finished the song with his arms around two of the dancing girls.

The curtain fell and rose again several times until the very final bow, after which he released the dancers more abruptly than they expected. They trotted to the back of the stage. Arms reached out for him, and hands patted his back, but he barely acknowledged them. His feelings were far too raw to share his colleagues' bonhomie during the post-show buffet, no matter how well-meaning their intentions were.

He walked on through the semi-darkness between the rear curtains and out through a fire door. The auditorium had been hot, so the cooler night air rasped in his throat. With the rainbow lights still blurring his vision and the music dying away in his ears, Norman felt slightly disorientated. A dog barked in the alley, making him jump. Seeing no one about, he hotfooted it across the street to where he had parked his car. It was a deliberately chosen spot, half-hidden against a wall just off the main road. He threw his coat over most of his face, hoping he could get to it without being pestered. He stepped out of the alley, got halfway down the road, when he suddenly felt a sharp jab in his ribs. He swung his arm up over his shoulder in the direction of the pain. It was grabbed by one of two assailants, the lower halves of whose bodies he managed to make out before a gloved hand was cupped over his face and his arm forced up behind his back.

'You keep schtum and you keep walking.'

He made a fist with his other hand and swore loudly, but the second assailant grabbed his free arm and a gag was looped and tightened over his mouth.

'Get straight in the van and no one gets hurt.'

A vehicle with blacked out windows slid to a halt in front of them. The door opened quietly. Despite his continued struggles, he was bundled into the back and held face down on the floor, where they blindfolded him before he was able to get a clear view of either of them. The door slammed shut and the gun that had jabbed him earlier was pushed hard into his back.

'Phone. Where's your phone?'

Norman worked out that the second assailant was doing the talking. His arms were released. His hands went straight to the tight gag, but they were snatched away from him and twisted behind his back once more. A fist struck the side of his head, and he cried out.

'That means you give us it now, old man.'

He gave a muffled gasp, and the van jerked away. They made him sit up, pushing the gun into his side again.

'I'll only ask politely one more time: hand over the phone or it starts to get uncomfortable.'

Norman's breath came heavily. One hand was released. He put it on his chest and leaned forward, gasping and panting. For a moment or two, no one reacted. The car cornered sharply, forcing Norman to put his free hand down to right himself. An arm went under his neck and pulled his head to one side. He put his hand into his coat pocket and produced his mobile phone.

'You can have it back when we let you go.'

The second assailant took it from him. Norman heard him fumble around for the off button. No one would be able to trace him now.

The vehicle cornered again the other way. Norman guessed they were going up the A10 and correctly anticipated a roundabout that put them on a winding road through the forest. So far, he was familiar with the route. He had been born in this part of the country and the forest had shaped his childhood. The villages dotted throughout its wooded bounds had assembly rooms, dance clubs, and church halls. Scantily-furnished venues such as these had faithfully nurtured his post-war comic routines.

The gun moved in his side. 'Cooperate and we won't keep you long.'

Norman let his arms fall into his lap. He sat very still, trying to appear compliant but all the while trying to work out where they were taking him. It became harder when they circled a roundabout several times, though he could tell by the sound of the van that they were going deeper into the forest. The vehicle reversed several times and he thought it went back some of the way it had come; either they were lost or they were trying to confuse him. The van picked up speed, and as they went round a tight corner he and his companion were thrown to one side. He made a grab for the blindfold, but going into the straight his hand was pushed down again, and the gun held against his head. He grunted, fighting for breath again.

He could only think of one road where it was possible to drive so fast. He regained control of his breathing, keeping as still as he could. He might be able to lead detectives to his captors… if he got out of this alive.

The vehicle stopped and a front window whirred open. A different voice, coming from outside, spoke.

'Fine, sir. If you'd like to park over on the left, I'll escort you across to the centre.'

'No.' As the voice came from in front of him, he assumed it was the driver. 'I'll go across to Area B, if it's all the same to you.'

'That's the Centre of Operations.'

'I know.'

Norman listened intently. He had no idea where he was.

'I can't give you clearance for the van.'

'I believe you can. Would you check these documents, please?'

The man stepped away from the vehicle and Norman heard snatches of a phone conversation. The engine hummed very quietly. The man returned.

'That seems to be in order, sir. If you'd just like to…' But before he had finished giving instructions, the window closed.

They drove slowly for a few yards, and then stopped with a jolt. The back door banged open and the gun-toting assailant got out. The side door slid back and Norman was pushed through. He would have fallen onto the concrete had the gunman not grabbed him, righted him, and stuck the gun in the middle of his back again. It clicked. The first assailant spoke close to his ear.

'If you want to get out of here quickly and safely then you walk straight ahead and you look straight ahead. Got it?'

As he suddenly felt the fight drain out of him, he simply nodded. The blindfold was removed. He saw he was standing in front of a half-open door. Goaded by the gun, he was frog-marched through it and down a corridor. The gag was ripped off.

'Where am I being taken?' he asked.

The second assailant said harshly, 'You're being taken to a little room, where you will show us how much you really love your country. You've sung about it often enough.'

He said nothing in reply. They walked through the dim light coming from windows above metal doors. Some had glass portholes at head height, but Norman made a point of not looking.

'Stop!'

This door had no such window. It opened from the other side and he was shoved through.

He stumbled into a brightly-lit computer suite. There were three people, two men and a woman. The woman sat facing away from him in front of two monitors. The men sat to her left, looking at him. He blinked hard. The computers beeped and squeaked as though infested by rodents.

'Good evening, Mr Bundle,' said the man in the middle of the three. 'I apologise for the mode of transport tonight, but we weren't in a position to make appointments. You can call me Baxter. This is Turner. We do the IT. Minerva here looks after the main console. She's more what you'd call management. All we need to do is interview you. I'm sure you're quite used to that.' He reached out his hand. Norman didn't shake it.

'My name's not Bundle, it's Brown... Norman Brown, as you well know.' One of the computers gave a single high-pitched squeal. He looked at it. 'Bundle is just my stage name.'

'Don't say "just", Mr Brown.'

'You'd better credit us with some intelligence,' said Minerva without turning round, 'so that we can all get on with our work.'

'Why have I been brought here?'

'We think you can probably guess,' said Turner. 'We've been having trouble with some of our systems.'

There was another squeal from the largest of the computers. This time it had an almost musical tone to it. Norman's brow furrowed.

'Since your brother hacked into them,' said Minerva. 'Only he's not your brother. Guess what? We knew that too.' Baxter looked hard at Minerva, but she ignored him.

'You killed Piggy Bundle?' Norman's voice quavered.

'No,' continued Baxter rising up out of his seat. 'He spotted our men following him, and he accelerated. There was nothing anyone could do. We didn't want him dead, that was the last thing we wanted.'

'He left a missus and three kiddies!'

'I know. I was furious, but as I say, there was nothing anyone could do. He hit the verge too fast. Our car wasn't anywhere near him when it happened. The lads were really upset about it.'

'You lot were upset! How do you think his family feels?'

'Let's get this over with. You've got to let us have the passwords and encryptions he used so we can sort out this mess. Then you're going to sign some forms, then go home, and that will be an end to it. I am sorry about Piggy.'

'Not his real name,' sneered Minerva.

Baxter turned to her. 'Take it easy. We need his help.'

She tensed her shoulders. The computer gave its longest squeak yet, ending in a smooth descent. Norman brushed his hand across his face in time with it. Turner rose and stood in front of the long desk that stretched the length of the room. He relaxed into a half-seated position.

'We need you to remove the malware and other stuff he's uploaded before we sweep for any other anomalies. There are errors on every sector, and we can't run a clean sweep until we're rid of them.'

Norman looked at him. There was another squeak. Norman glanced at the screen, then Turner, then the screen again.

Minerva spoke next, 'So, what about it then?'

'I couldn't if I wanted to,' said Norman. 'It's not my bag. Piggy was the computer man. I know he was doing something a bit out of the ordinary. I think he wanted something to make his puppets move. It was for the show, for the kiddies, you know. Me, I'm old-fashioned. I don't do computers, but I'll sing and dance for you, if you like.'

'You must know something,' said Baxter. 'Like where he keeps all his passwords? He's used our software, he must have got past our firewalls somehow.'

'I know he's got a computer. I could talk to his missus.'

Minerva swung round. 'She's there and you're here. Unless we bring her in too?'

'I said *I'll* talk to her! You leave her out of this!'

'All right, all right,' Baxter intervened. 'We've gone through all his online accounts and bank statements and drawn a blank. He knew what he was doing… What's the matter?'

Norman was staring at the noisy computer. 'That noise… is that to do with Piggy?'

Minerva swivelled her chair towards Turner. 'Run the Loop Analyser,' she snapped.

Sine waves appeared on the screen. 'Is this the sound?' Turner asked.

Norman nodded. 'Yep. That's what I heard.'

Turner froze the loop and wound back to the waveform that described the most recent noise. He greyed out its entire shape, selected "Search" from the drop-down menu, then sat back and waited as the algorithm compared it with a bank of other sounds.

'I'll tell you this,' said Norman, 'Piggy wasn't into any of that sort of stuff. A few cartoons maybe, but not that.'

'Right,' said Turner as the results appeared on the screen. He ran a tracing programme to find the source. 'Now listen again.'

Baxter and Minerva watched intently. White lines flashed on the screen and the room filled with a white noise that gradually mutated into the squeaks that had perturbed Norman so much.

An orange spot appeared.

Norman froze. 'It... it c-c-can't be,' he stuttered.

Another orange spot. His eyes darted to it.

'Believe us, it can.' Turner clicked the mouse while Baxter watched Norman's transfixed expression.

The spots turned to blobs and then coalesced into one orange mass. Norman stood up and stumbled back from the screen.

'Hold him steady, Baxter.'

The mass divided into two discrete parts: upper and lower.

Norman pointed at Baxter, then at Turner. 'Is this why you've bought me here?'

Suddenly, two black triangles materialised on the upper section. Norman's jaw dropped.

'Give him some water,' said Baxter.

Turner looked for the jug that was always kept behind the console. Norman had turned white.

'Get away! I don't want water. I can't believe this!' He pointed a shaking finger at the screen and his voice quavered. 'It's... it's... No! Yes!'

The water jug wasn't there. Maybe someone had moved it.

'Go on, tell us! It's his work, isn't it?' snapped Baxter as the comedian knelt in front of the console.

'It is!' He reached forward as though expecting his arms to pass through the screen.

'What's he doing?' asked Minerva.

Norman was shaking. 'It really is!' he cried. 'It's Sooty!'

The two computer scientists looked at one another. Minerva sniffed. 'A glove puppet from years ago? Really!'

They helped Norman into a chair. Minerva found the water and poured it into a mug.

'It is... and it isn't,' said Norman as he took a drink.

The individual elements had settled into the shape of a small orange bear with black ears; its arms as wide apart as a priest at the offertory.

'You see, he's got legs. At last! Isn't that amazing? I never thought I'd live to see this day.'

'It's using up all our processing power,' said Baxter, 'and because it constantly jumps from sector to sector, we can never fix on it.'

'Of course he does,' answered Norman. 'Of course he jumps! He's got legs! This is fantastic! Oh, my word! Look, he's doing a little dance!'

'Yeah,' said Minerva, 'and it's still messing up our data as it has done for months.'

'But,' said Norman, 'consider the implications for light entertainment!'

Baxter looked Norman squarely in the face. 'We have scrambled fighter jets to intercept non-existent Russian incursions into our airspace. We have misinformed NATO about the positions of Chinese spy satellites and we've nearly invaded half of Scandinavia. It's cost us tens of millions of pounds as well as jeopardised relations with the few Middle Eastern allies that we have left!'

The puppet stopped gyrating. Its arms moved inwards and its head tilted forward. More squeaks followed. Minerva threw an agitated glance towards her two colleagues.

'What's that all about? asked Turner.

Norman folded his arms. 'Sooty says he wants all the boys and girls to know he's very, very sorry, and he promises never to do it again.'

Baxter grabbed his shoulder. 'Norman,' he said, 'this is wrecking the very heart of our defence operations. It's going to leave us wide open to foreign interference... military intervention. It could be disastrous for the country you say you love.'

Norman stared at the small orange bear.

'Still,' he said wistfully, 'we may be the first humans to witness Sooty's legs.'

'You'd better do something about it,' growled Minerva. 'If you want to get out of here.'

Norman shrugged. 'As I said, I'm the old-fashioned one, I don't do... hang on! Oh, now look! He's got his magic wand as well!'

'I can't take any more of this,' sighed Minerva. 'We're wasting our time.'

Norman raised his arm. 'I might be able to help. I'll need some stuff though.'

'Tell us what you want,' said Turner. 'We'll get it. Don't worry.'

'Right then, first we'll need a top hat... on the screen, I mean... for him.'

Minerva and Baxter looked at each other. 'A top hat?' said Baxter.

Turner started tapping the keyboard. 'The Gamma Relay programme came with a virtual Monopoly game,' he said. 'One of the playing pieces happens to be a virtual top hat.'

'Funny you should know that,' said Minerva.

'I acquaint myself with every aspect of all the intelligence tools,' said Turner as he continued to tap. 'It's my job.'

'Have you ever played it?' asked Baxter.

There was a pause.

'Yes.'

The top hat was uploaded and set up on the screen next to the bear.

'Now, Sooty,' said Norman, 'I want you to do your famous disappearing act: the one you do at the end of your show.'

More squeaks emanated from the console.

'What does that mean?' asked Baxter.

'Sooty will only do his disappearing trick if all the boys and girls say the magic words. You'll have to lend me a pen.'

Minerva's gaze burned at Turner. Baxter gave Norman a pen and a sheet of paper. He wrote something on it and held it up to them.

'Come on then,' said Norman. 'All sit in a line.'

Minerva sat in the middle with Baxter and Turner on either side. Norman held up the sheet so they could read what he had scrawled.

'Izzy wizzy,' they chorused, 'let's get busy!'

Sooty tapped the hat three times with his wand.

'Ping!'

He had gone. Only an inverted top hat was left in view.

Norman clapped. 'Wowee,' he said. 'Now you can cut and paste the hat onto a USB stick for me to...'

Baxter interrupted, 'Delete.'

'You can't do that!'

'Delete.'

A simple click from Turner and the hat was gone.

'That was Piggy's life's work!'

'Get him out of here,' said Minerva, 'before I go mad. And tell Hood he can come in now.'

Baxter opened the door. The assailants who had abducted him were still outside. The man called Hood walked in between them. He was unshaven and wore a dark jacket over a colourful shirt. His gun hung half in and half out of his trouser pocket.

'I want all of those sectors cleaned up,' ordered Hood. 'I want you to sweep out every part of our nerve centre. Minerva, can you make sure it's all swept? We need everything swept thoroughly before we can reboot. There should be a command somewhere. I want it swept, swept, and swept again. Have you got that?'

As he was led away, Norman heard every word of Minerva's reply, yet he chose to say nothing.

'It's on this drop-down menu,' she said. 'Here we go. "Activate Sweep".'

2. THE GIRL WITH THE SILVER BULLET BRACELET

Eileen O'Rourke had gone back home. It was the first time she had returned since falling out with her mother six years previously following a period of intense acrimony. This, however, was no reconciliation. Her mother had just died, and now she had to clear out her place before the new tenants arrived. Those final bitter exchanges with her late mother still rankled. It was too soon for her to decide whether she regretted not having made up with her. Hilary, a childhood friend, had kept suggesting she should try to build bridges. Hilary was a churchgoer of sorts.

Eileen had never known a time when her mother hadn't been difficult to deal with. She had been a disturbed, chaotic woman, as unpredictable as she was recalcitrant. Being her only daughter, Eileen felt her entire childhood had been nothing but one big compromise, and for which she had Hilary's sympathy and agreement.

'So what's with the bullet?' asked Hilary as they filled cardboard boxes with her late mother's belongings to take to the charity shop.

'It was either the last or the only thing my father ever gave her.'

'Oh dear!'

Eileen grimaced, and held up a bracelet from which the bullet dangled. 'See? That's his name engraved on the side.'

'David O'Rourke?'

'That was him. Possibly still is, for all I know.' She laughed lightly.

'Does it fit you? Not that you'd want to wear it.'

Eileen wrapped it around her wrist. It fitted easily.

'There it is,' she said. In a moment of passing melancholy, she recalled that she had the same body proportions as her mother: breasts, feet, and even her fingers. Perhaps it was time to forgive. 'I'll keep it, I think. There's a little clasp on the side so I can take the bullet off if it gets too heavy.'

There wasn't much else she wanted to keep. Hilary took a couple of the glass ornaments and then boxed up the remaining clothes for the charity shop. Sadly, most of the trappings of that stressful, all-too-short life were destined for the recycling depot.

'You should try to find him,' said Hilary. 'Your father, I mean. He probably doesn't know she's died.'

Eileen was kneeling over a box. 'If he is still alive, he probably wouldn't care. Not if you believe all the stuff mother said about him.'

'Is he likely not to be alive?'

'He was a drinker, apparently. I never knew him.' She looked up, as though surprised by her own candour, and shook her rich black hair over her shoulders. She was a thin woman in her early thirties, with long eyelashes and lips that tended towards a boyish grin at the least provocation. Though dressed in a rough denim that gave the impression she was careless about her appearance, her clothes fitted the curves and angles of her fluid form with an almost sculptured smoothness.

Hilary, whose scruffiness suited her like a splash in a muddy river, grinned broadly. 'That's men for you!'

'Oh, no. I think he was special... in a bad way, I mean.'

Eileen had no memory of her father. All she had heard were the unsavoury stories her mother had told her, which she sensed were one-sided, even at a young age. This had caused most of their arguments. Once she had gone as far as threatening to track him down. That was when she had been shown the silver bullet bracelet. It had made quite an impression on her when she was young.

Eileen was glad when the house clearance was done and dusted. Hilary drove her to the train station, and she managed to get back to her bedsit before October's early dusk.

When she got in, she discovered one of her colleagues had dropped off some forms from the learning support team that was based at the local school. She worked there as a teaching assistant three days a week. She also had a text from Rick inviting her out for a drink.

Rick was a friend she had made in the local pub. She thought he was a sweet man. As she flopped onto her bed to read through the forms, she realised she was still wearing the bracelet. She twisted it between her finger and thumb till she found the clasp. It unclipped easily, and she placed it carefully on the bedside table. While she read through the forms, she found herself glancing at it from time to time. It was quirky. She liked quirky objects. She decided to wear it for school. Perhaps it would be nice to have that one memento of her mother on her at all times… or that one memento of having had a mother. She snorted grimly.

*****

Eileen put the bracelet on that night when she went to The County Arms for a drink.

'It's very different,' said Rick when she showed it to him. He gulped his lager. 'You could start a new trend in fashionable weaponry.'

'Very funny.'

'No. But have you ever thought of finding him?'

'I have,' she said. 'It would be complicated because he isn't on my birth certificate. By the time I was born, she

15

hated him so much that she wouldn't admit to even knowing who my father was.'

'Just go on social media.'

'I can't.' The school had advised its staff, and particularly support staff, to avoid social media as some of the more challenging pupils were able to hack into accounts for nefarious reasons. Eileen didn't use social media, and she didn't like computers much anyway.

'If you want me to help you, I can. Or you could pay a detective.'

'A detective! I'm not that bothered about him. I'd just like to know how bad he really was. I know my mother couldn't have made up everything she said about him. She wasn't imaginative enough for one thing.'

*****

The funeral took place a week later in the local crematorium. Eileen knew that some of the neighbours had been acquainted with her, but couldn't think of any who actually liked her. Nevertheless, she put a note through their doors and left it up to them. None came. Eileen and Hilary were the only two members in the congregation.

Afterwards, the two young women went to The County Arms and drank Irish whiskey in honour of the lately deceased. The barman commiserated and complimented Eileen on the bracelet.

'She once had a nice brooch that I would have liked as well,' she told him. 'But I think she must have sold it... or pawned it, more likely.'

'Well, things could have been worse for her. It was quite a nice little house,' said Hilary. 'Local authority, wasn't it? Otherwise, the rent would have been ridiculous, when you think of round here.'

'I don't know. I doubt if she ever paid any rent knowing her.'

The area around the station had become gentrified over the past thirty years. However, the local council remained stoically supportive of lower income groups and encouraged small developers rather than large conglomerates. As a result, the housing stock was more suited to young families and because of this, people didn't move away in droves, as they did in other parts of London.

*****

Rick liked Eileen. More than liked her. So did a lot of men. It wasn't just that she was attractive; she also had a vivaciousness that bordered on the reckless, particularly after a drink or two. He liked to walk her home when she was in one of her silly moods, although she never invited him in for a nightcap. But Rick hadn't given up, and her interest in tracking her father offered him a way into her favours.

In his work as a carpenter, he used computers to produce designs that were clear enough to convince prospective customers. Because he worked for himself, he was able to spend the greater part of the morning researching the "Eileen: Father" project on his laptop.

The limited information that Eileen had (a time, a place, a trade, and the name "O'Rourke") led him to a building site in South London. Having none of Eileen's reticence towards social media, he was able to pinpoint a number of builders who might have worked there. He then narrowed the search down to a few who were old enough to have been on-site at the same time as his man. After a few blind alleys, he homed in on a likely suspect. His time-consuming investigations had taken him round the peripheral enough times to realise that he was onto something at last. In the end, he had to resort to a private detective to get the man's personal details: something he would never tell Eileen. Nor would he tell her about any of the lengths he had gone to. That she would be both grateful and impressed was enough for Rick, particularly the latter!

He was given an address on a housing estate served by a pub called The Greyhound. His mate Barry knew it. Barry, an expert at the quiz machines, knew all the pubs in the area. Every Friday, he, Rick, and latterly Eileen met in The County Arms for an evening of drinks and challenges.

'It's not a very salubrious area,' said Barry, a builder by trade, who mostly worked for himself like Rick. 'I wouldn't wander round there on my own, night or day.'

Barry worked out in a gym twice a week, and Rick recalled that he used to do judo or some similar martial art. If six-foot Barry Myers wouldn't go there, then Rick wasn't sure he wanted to pass the details on to Eileen.

'Have you been there before?'

'I know the pub,' Barry said. 'It's a bad place: drugs, prostitution, gangs, you name it. You probably wouldn't even get served. The police keep it open because it keeps the lousiest items in one place. If her old man lives out there, she really is best shot of him. I wouldn't like to tell her that though.'

*****

Rick didn't see Eileen again until the following week. When he didn't immediately volunteer the results of his research, she asked him. Despite warning her about the nature of the place, she still wanted to know.

'I might not even go round there,' she reassured him. 'I just want to know where he is so I could write or something. I could let him know about Mum. Have you seen his name is engraved on the side of this?' She held up her bracelet.

'I see. That's quite funny.'

'I wonder if he did it or she did it.' She said it in such a matter of fact way that, unexpectedly, it seemed hard to imagine that her mother wasn't at home waiting for her that very moment. Perhaps Hilary was right: maybe she should have attempted a reconciliation with her mother.

'I can only just make it out,' said Rick. 'The lettering must have got rubbed down by wear. I guess she must have worn it quite a lot.'

'If she ever did, I don't remember.'

'Maybe he gave it to her as a threat or something nasty like that.'

'I don't know.' She had considered that possibility. 'Anyway,' she took the piece of paper with the address from him, 'I'll have to decide what to do about this information.'

'Be very careful,' he warned.

Rick knew Eileen was doing well in her school. Not everyone wanted to work with troubled teenagers, but he enjoyed listening to her success stories and could tell she loved her job. A piece of excellent writing, the discovery of a facility for maths, a homework that went beyond expectation or even an unlikely reconciliation with a member of staff; she would offer these as small victories: not to flaunt her own virtue but as a genuine expression of her unaffected joy at the resilience of humanity.

However, a feisty determination and smart repartee wouldn't protect her from the thugs on the Belamy Estate. Rick's last foray there had been to replace the kitchen in a house where seven members of a family had fallen victim to a psychopathic arsonist. The thought of it made him shudder, so he phoned Barry the following day.

'Why did you have to tell her you'd found him?' Barry asked. 'You could've lied.'

'She probably would've traced him anyway. It wasn't that difficult.'

'But then it wouldn't have been your fault if anything happened.'

'We could offer to go with her.'

'We?'

'You're a bit more useful than me in certain respects.'

'I'll go with her, not you. You'd be a liability, mate. I'll be in The County tomorrow; we'll have a chat with her then.'

Rick's weekly alcoholic intake had increased in line with his patronage of that establishment simply because Eileen regularly went there. With Barry's incursion, he felt the opportunity to act as her mentor had been snatched away from him.'

Eileen had a surprise for them.

'I don't know what you're both making such a fuss about,' she said. 'I've already been. I finished a bit early today, so I walked round there. It was still daylight, I was fine.'

'What was he like?' asked Barry.

Barry always dressed very neatly. He wore expensive trousers and silk shirts in a variety of shimmering colours. When he sat on a barstool, his knees would open to either side because of his bulk.

'He wasn't in,' she said. 'I just saw where he lived.'

'What did the house look like then?'

'It's just a mobile home. You go to a gate at the end of the estate, and there's this bit of wasteland, I suppose that's what it is, and there are all these mobile homes on it. I think it's called Wildens. It looked a bit neglected. That's all really.'

'I think I might have seen those mobile homes,' said Barry. 'If it's the place I'm thinking of, it's in a pretty bad state, or it was back then.'

Eileen bought their next drinks. 'There you are,' she said. 'My two brave protectors.'

'I thought Wildens might have been the name of his house,' said Rick disappointedly.

'Well, it obviously wasn't,' said Barry. 'How did you know which mobile home was his?'

'I asked someone,' she said.

'I'm impressed,' said Barry. She smiled at him.

Rick frowned. 'I'm not! They're a bad lot out there. Anything could have happened.' And to emphasise his concern, he took a deep draught of his pint of beer.

Barry laughed. 'She knows these people, Rick. She teaches their kiddies!'

'I do,' she said. 'Anyway, the man who showed me round was quite well spoken.'

'You mean he didn't eff and blind every other word.'

'No! His name was Deano. He was a big fellow. You wouldn't want to cross him!'

Rick finished his beer and got himself another half. The others didn't want any more to drink.

'I still say we go with you next time,' he said. But Barry and Eileen were deep in conversation. After they left, he stayed on to finish his beer, then walked home feeling down.

*****

The next time Rick saw Eileen, he was surprised to hear that she hadn't been back to the mobile home.

'I took the bracelet into Ron's, that little place on the road that goes past the bus station. The man said he'd clean it up and do something about the engraving. It's a real bullet, by the way, and the bracelet is silver.'

'You should have taken it to the jewellers.'

'I did, but they didn't want to know. Snobs! I want to have it when I next go over there. You know, just in case I see him.'

'When you go, Eileen, do you mind if I come with you? I know you've already been round there, but Barry is a bit worried. You know what he's like. I think he'd like to know you were in safe hands.'

'It's really my business. What would the man think if I came with a minder?'

'You could say we were in a relationship.'

'We aren't.' She spoke abruptly, as if pre-empting any possibility that there ever would be. His expression clouded. She relented. 'I'll tell you what, perhaps you could hang back and keep a lookout for me. How about that? Perhaps Barry could join you, too. Then we could all have a drink after.'

'I don't know if Barry would want to.'

*****

Eileen phoned Rick as soon as she got the bracelet back. They met at the top of the hill that divided the north and south of the village. He had printed out a map from the internet, but it didn't have the mobile home park on it so she had to pencil it in for him. He got her to mark the position of O'Rourke's abode as best as she could remember.

'He doubtless drinks in The Greyhound,' he said ominously as they walked on down towards the shops.

There was a triangle, where buses paused or stopped, just as the steepest rise levelled out. As the late afternoon light began to fade, the pair of them walked past a line of shops before coming to a criss-crossing of terraced streets interlaced with tall Edwardian buildings, most of which had been divided into flats and allowed to decay. The Belamy Estate blended in with them further ahead.

'I can't say I'm not feeling nervous,' she said, 'but I do want to handle this myself.'

'Fair enough. I'll follow at a distance. I'll phone you after, say, half an hour.'

She walked down a long road towards a gate fixed to a brick wall by a single rusty hinge that had solidified with disuse. The lush undergrowth beneath showed that the gate had not been closed for years. Rick waited till she was out of sight, then he followed slowly.

The mobile homes were low and narrow. Each one had a tiny kitchen on the side nearest the path. The first few groups were arranged in neat rows and seemed well kept with colourful curtains bunched to the sides of their windows. Some of the curtains were closed, although the flickering light of a television was still visible. Further in and the layout became less regular, higgledy-piggledy even, as if the towmaster who had hauled them in had become more blasé the further he had to drag them. There was more rubbish on the paths and grass verges until, right at the very end, there was no path at all.

Twilight was falling, and she had to get close to the door to check that she had the right number. There was no doorbell or knocker, and the interior was dimly lit: the glow proceeding from a window to the side of her. She could hear voices, but they seemed to come from behind. She waited. People were coming. She pushed herself flat against the door and, again from behind, heard the sound of a shout and a scuffle. She froze. Silence. She took out her phone and stared down at the tiny numbers. Before she had time to call, the door suddenly opened, and she nearly fell in.

'What the hell do you want?'

'I…'

A fist grabbed her by the hair and pulled her in. As she fell onto the bare fibreglass floor, her phone slid out of reach. She looked up and saw an angular face. It was frighteningly similar to hers but for missing teeth and a grossly misshapen nose. His checked shirt was torn to the elbow, and he wore unbuckled sandals. His bare feet, like his fists and face, were brown and asymmetrical. He smelt of whiskey.

'Get up then! Get up, I said!'

She pushed herself away from him and sat up against the door. Her head hurt where she had banged it on landing. 'I came to see you.'

'You came to see me the other day. Now you've broken into my home. If I kill you, it counts as self-defence. You'd know that if you read your newspapers. Who sent you?'

'No one sent me.' She spat out the words. Any thoughts of dignifying this monster with the knowledge that he was her father were draining away.

'Let me go!'

He punched her so hard in the side of the chest that she felt her ribs crack.

'Tell me who you're working for.'

She gasped for air as he aimed for her again. The force of the blow broke the door causing her to fall backwards, her head hitting the gravel outside. The taste of blood was thick in her mouth. As she reached for something to steady herself, her hands touched a shiny black boot. It curled under her neck, propelling her back into the mobile home. The unconscious frame of Rick tumbled in soon after. She painfully creased open her eyes and recognised the owner of the boot.

'Deano!' she gasped at the tall Afro-Caribbean man who had delivered her companion. Dressed in a waistcoat and dark chinos, his wide eyes bore down on her with fire.

'I'll get them into the next room,' said Deano. 'You'd better scout around to see if there are any more skulking about.'

'I'll do that, sir. I'll do that right away,' said her father.

Eileen tried to get up, but Deano held her by the wrist in a powerful grip. She tried to get some traction with her feet as he dragged her into the middle, and largest, of the three rooms into which the interior was divided. Once in, she was sent sprawling face first onto the floor, where she choked on her own blood and spittle. Dazed and aching, she rolled over and saw that the walls were completely covered with posters of wrestlers, and flyers for wrestling matches and other sports events. The only furniture was a wooden chair and a cabinet. It certainly hadn't been laid out with any creature comforts in mind. She lay there terrified and sick. Then Rick was thrown in, almost on top of her.

'I don't think your friend is very well,' said Deano in the soft, mannered voice she had heard when he directed her to the mobile home a week previously. 'Now, why don't you tell me who you are working for?'

'Nobody,' she said, hauling herself up. 'You'd better let me go.'

'Oh, I can't do that. I want to know more about you.'

Eileen was dizzy and aching. Rick was still unconscious; she couldn't tell if he was breathing. She felt his chest. Deano sat down and undid the cabinet. He took out a gun.

'Oh, for God's sake!' said Eileen. He leaned forward. The muzzle was about a foot away from her head. 'You want to know why I came. He's my father!'

He tilted the gun down so she could watch him pull back the hammer. He aimed it at her and grinned, his green eyes glittering. 'A prodigal daughter,' he said. 'I don't see that we need prodigals around here.' His grin hardened and he aimed the gun directly at her forehead. He moved his head in concentration and pulled the trigger. The hammer fell into place with a click. She screamed, and he burst out laughing. Sobbing, she lay protectively across Rick's chest as he groaned. 'You're mad!' she said.

'It's an antique,' he said, wiping his eyes. 'There's no way I'd let David keep a real gun. He'd get us all sent down! No, this is an old Rosenthal. You don't see these any more. David got it from an auction. I think they stopped making ammunition for these in… let's see… '73 or something.' He put it back in the cabinet as David returned.

'I didn't see anyone else around,' said David, coming into the room. 'I don't know what's going on here. I haven't said anything, Deano… not to anyone. So if they say I have, then they're lying. You know that?' He was carrying a bottle of whiskey. Eileen put her elbows on the floor and propped herself up.

'Meet your daughter,' said Deano.

'My daughter?'

'So she says.'

David looked closely at her, and she winced. 'I heard there was a girl. So she grew up to be a housebreaker then. Got herself and her friend killed breaking in.'

'We didn't break in.' Rick had come round and was sitting up with blood running down the side of his face. 'We came to see you, like she said. We came because your ex-wife has died.'

'Maggie's died then.' David took a long pull on his whiskey. 'Well now, there's a thing.'

There was a long pause. Eileen could hear the metal hull of the mobile home creak as Deano shifted his weight.

'If we use our brains here,' said Deano, 'I think we can all agree there's been a misunderstanding. After all,' he addressed Eileen, 'it seemed to us like a break-in.'

'I'm sorry. We're both sorry.' said Eileen. 'Now let us go.'

Deano's phone buzzed. 'I've got business,' he said. 'Much as I would like to stay and enjoy this family reunion,

I'm going to leave you to handle this. Do you think you can sort this out, David?'

'Yes, sir. I think so.'

'I don't think we need another mess. Find out where they live and walk them off this private land.'

'No mess this time,' said David, nodding vigorously. Deano jumped up and hurried out into the night.

'Let us go and we won't come back,' said Eileen.

'Not so fast,' said David. 'You say Maggie is dead now, so there must be an inheritance. I guess some of it must be mine. We were married, after all.'

'She left nothing!' Eileen's courage returned with her anger. 'You gave her nothing but your drunken brutality!' As she raged at him, Rick surreptitiously pulled out his phone. David put down his bottle on the cabinet and kicked him; his sandal-clad toe connected with Rick's chin, making him yell. David snatched the phone, opened the cabinet, and retrieved a small hammer. He went outside, locking them in on the way. Through the window, she could see David bashing the phone to pieces and swearing as he did so. He came back into the mobile home still swearing, but the drink had affected him so much that he struggled to unlock the door. When he finally made it into the room, he saw Rick sitting in the chair with Eileen standing next to him and holding the gun. A broad grin crept across his face.

'I found it in your cabinet,' she said.

'You have my gun! Oh, as you can see, I am so scared.' He raised his hands. 'Guns are bad things. The trouble is, they always need loading.'

She ducked behind the cabinet, grabbed the whiskey bottle and threw it at him. He caught it deftly by the neck and drained it. 'One last drink for the condemned man.' He smashed the empty bottle on the floor.

'Stay back,' she warned him. 'I'll use it!'

'I think you should.' He made fists of his hands and lurched towards her.

She pulled the trigger. The hammer fell into place with a bang. He clutched his chest and stumbled, bleeding, to his knees. The look of surprise that formed during the few seconds it took him to fall froze on his face.

'That bullet had your name on it,' she said.

3. CHRISTINE

Children were playing noisily along the terraced street where Colin Bolton lived, but he didn't mind. They kicked balls against walls, shot basketballs through a hoop attached to a fencepost, and rode their bicycles down the little alleyways. Their high-pitched shouts echoed into the sparse gardens that backed onto them. As most of the residents had children, the road in front of the terrace became a playground. Sleeping policemen and the new 20mph signs put up by council forced traffic to drive slowly along this communal space. Not everybody liked the activity, but Colin found it cheerfully distracting. Nearing the end of his higher training, he had been given a placement with a top consultant psychiatrist, so his plans to move to a more rural area had to stay on hold for a little longer. He loved his work, and, for now, he liked his tiny house from where he was able to cycle to the clinic. He also loved his footie on the telly.

'Ah Colin... Couldn't do my last appointment for me today, could you, mate?'

George Weldon, MBBS, CCST, FRCPsych, CCT, PhD ran the practice. He oversaw the personnel development programme and enjoyed watching the raw trainees grow into skilled practitioners.

'It's been full on today, George.'

'You'll be home in time for the match.'

'Well...'

'It's Marsha Bell. She's pretty much on the way to recovery, so there's really nothing much to do. She hardly needs us now. These last sessions are just box-ticking for the Probation Service.'

'All right then. OK.'

'Thanks, mate, I owe you one… Sorry, got to rush to get to that emergency Parole Board hearing. I'm late already!'

Colin agreed to see her partly because he could still get home in time to watch the match (Chelsea was playing Wolverhampton and Mourinho's team was in big trouble, to say the least) and partly because Marsha was an interesting case. Her recovery had progressed at a remarkable pace since George Weldon had been working with her. George always said he worked "with" someone rather than "on" or "for", as if they were part of his team. Colin wondered whether that really happened or whether it was just something he said to make his patients believe they had ownership of their recovery.

Marsha suffered psychotic episodes in which she experienced things that weren't there. She saw her hallucinations as clearly as one person sees another. Colin's curiosity was aroused because, so far, he hadn't come across anyone like her.

Marsha, a small prim lady with wavy hair dyed a deep brown, was sitting in a chair in the waiting room. She wore a green, flowery dress that gracefully covered her knees. After introducing himself, Colin led her into the office. As expected, there was the obligatory psychiatrist's couch, but the only people who lay on it were those who thought that was what one had to do. Marsha sat with her hands folded in her lap while he went through the usual pleasantries.

'Looking through the notes, I can see that you are, to all intents and purposes, recovered. So really, if there's anything you want to ask me or tell me, then fire away, Marsha.'

'No, there's nothing. I only have two more sessions after this and then that's it. I have to attend them all because of my probation rules.'

30

He shuffled his notes.

'Sorry, of course. Umm… we don't have to make this a long session.'

'No.'

'So, I see here that you saw a person.'

'A person?'

He coughed behind his hand. 'An hallucination.'

'I don't any more. I take the pills and I don't get that anymore.' Her hands moved to the arms of the chair and her elbows bent.

'No. I know, and that's good… that's great. It was a female, wasn't it.'

'It was.'

'What sort of female?'

'It was a young girl… Look, can we drop this? You're making me stressed!'

'No, no… yes, sure… I mean, of course. It must have been really upsetting for you.'

'It was, but I don't have it any more. I'm cured, have you got that? Mr Weldon says so, and I've only got two more sessions left. You know I'm back at work, don't you?'

Things seemed to go downhill after that. Everything Colin said seemed to make her bridle. By the end of the session, she was barely audible as she sat hunched up in the chair, her knees clasped against her chest. When Colin eventually brought the meeting to a close, she left without a word.

*****

'How did Chelsea do the other day?' George asked him the following week. George was good at keeping relationships sweet with his colleagues, especially when he had to offer honest criticism.

'They lost. A penalty.'

'Not good... Not for Mourinho anyway!'

'You're right, it wasn't!'

'Colin, I had a chat with Marsha's probation officer, and he said she was all over the place after Wednesday's session. What happened there?'

'I don't know. I think I just lost my way a bit with the conversation.'

'D'you wanna talk about it?'

'Not really. I know where it went wrong. It won't happen again.'

That small aberration that had occurred when she was with Colin could simply be put down to a clash of personalities. It happens in all professions. That was why it was so good to work in a practice. Even the easy-going George Weldon occasionally came across patients who didn't get on with him, and he usually passed these cases on to colleagues, who often achieved spectacular results. There was never any acrimony: everyone has different needs and different skills. Perhaps Colin still needed to learn patience and humility. George felt he had a tendency to be a bit over-competitive.

'Good. These things happen from time to time. Psychiatry isn't an exact science, if it's a science at all! I'll leave you to get things straight with her because I'm off all day on Wednesday.'

No one likes to screw up at work, and Colin was still on edge when he arrived home that evening. As he supported his bike in one hand and searched his pockets with the other for his key, he leaned against the front door. It opened unexpectedly, and he tumbled into the hallway with the bike on top of him. He disentangled himself and, fearing he had been burgled, cautiously went inside.

Standing in his living room was a curly-haired child wearing a checked shirt and jeans. Colin began to shake. A tremor that started in his shoulders and then moved down his body. The girl grinned and pointed a finger at him in the manner of a cowboy holding a gun.

'What are you doing? Get out!' he yelled.

'It was open.' She laughed, dancing past him.

Colin hunched his shoulders, watching her disappear into a group of children that had suddenly appeared from the alley.

Had he left the door open?

He spent an hour checking that nothing was missing, going through all his cupboards and shelves. Then he microwaved a frozen stew that tasted of cardboard and made him feel sick. He didn't sleep very well that night, and the following day he had a headache.

'Are you still OK with Marsha tomorrow?' asked George kindly. 'I can alter things if not.'

'No, I'll be fine. I'd like to know a few more details about the case, though. I think that would help.'

'It should all be in the notes.'

'I mean about her visions... that girl she kept seeing. What did she look like?'

'I don't want you to go there with that stuff. She's over it, and you run the risk of re-awakening it. It's not important now.'

Colin narrowed his mouth. 'I'll steer clear then.'

'That's the ticket. If you really want to know, her hallucinations were of a child. She called her "Christine".'

*****

Colin was as good as his word and Marsha's penultimate session was mostly a matter of protocol for the sake of her probation. It was Marsha who brought up the subject of her problem by comparing how she felt in the present to the recent past. Colin reassured her.

'And your life will continue to improve, that's the way with these things. No more Christines, eh?'

If he had taken a few steps forward in gaining her confidence, then he was aware that he had suddenly taken as many steps back on mentioning Christine. For a few minutes, she clammed up, scowling in an ugly manner. The end of the session was hard work, but Colin felt satisfied with it. He spent a good hour writing it up.

It was dusk, when he cycled into his road, which was unusually quiet. All the children must have been indoors, and he was glad not to see them as he stopped pedalling, the bike rolling on under its own momentum.

'Hallo, Colin.'

'Jesus!' He put an unsteady foot on the ground and turned to see the same girl. It was her; he recognised the checked shirt. She put her hands on her hips and leaned forward towards him, giggling. He nearly fell over.

'Get away!' he shouted.

She shrieked and ran down the alley. He ought to complain to the parents or phone the police. He felt that strange tremor in his body again. He was still shaking as he entered the house. He picked up the newspaper that had been stuffed through his letterbox and sat reading it in his chair. He turned straight to the sports pages. More about Mourinho. Chelsea was playing Manchester United. Not good news; although without Ferguson, Man U wasn't the team it used to be.

He suddenly slammed the paper down. All the books on the shelf had been pulled out, two of the drawers were open, and there was a bottle opener was on the floor. Now, he really should call the police, but first he wanted to find out how the intruder had got in. He checked the windows: they were all locked. The back door was secure, and he knew he had carefully locked the front door that morning when he left the house. He had made a point of double-checking the locks ever since that day he had found it open.

He rummaged around in the drawers. Nothing was missing. What could he tell the police? He would look silly. Maybe he had left everything in this state? But he couldn't have... wouldn't have. His head swam, and the aching resumed.

He saw the girl again the following day: she was watching him from the alley. Then, at the weekend, she stepped out in front of him as he was walking back home with his shopping. He nearly tripped over. Once more, she found his discomfiture screamingly funny. He didn't.

He quickly dumped the shopping outside his front door and followed her. If he could find out who her friends were, he might be able to track down a parent, but she disappeared into a crowd of children as before. He couldn't distinguish which one she was, so he had to give up.

She did it again on Monday: calling his name, and then disappearing. On Tuesday, she was standing bold as brass by his front door.

'Who are you?' he said.

As she ran off, screaming with spiteful laughter, he could have sworn he heard her say "Christine".

Perhaps he shouldn't have gone into work on Wednesday. He made mistakes with the paperwork, double-booked an appointment, and snapped at a senior consultant who was visiting George.

Colin looked drawn.

'Take the afternoon off, mate,' said George.

'No, really... I'm fine.'

'You don't look it.'

'Just a bit stressed, but I'm seeing my folks next weekend, so I'll get some rest then.' George nodded.

'I'll tell you what, mate, pints at lunchtime. I've only got Marsha this morning. It's her last session. Come and celebrate a success story with me. Remember, you had a part in it too.' Colin downed the dregs of his coffee, gripping the cup with his teeth.

*****

In common with many creatures, we are equipped with mirror neurons in our brains that enable us to empathise with others and to hone the delicate skills required for lacework or brain surgery. Empathy is a psychiatrist's bread-and-butter, but this can leave them open to inadvertently copying the emotions or traits of their patients. Unfortunately, when this happens, the psychiatrists themselves are usually the last to know.

The interview was merely a formality, and George only spent half an hour with Marsha, mostly filling in forms. She told him about her new job and how pleased her probation officer was. She was completely relaxed; glad to have George run the session again, no doubt. He and Colin could nip off a bit earlier to the pub for lunch and a chat. Nice one.

The session came to a speedy and satisfactory end.

'That's it, Marsha,' he said. 'Unless there's anything you want to ask me?'

'No, no,' she smiled. 'You've been very helpful.'

'You can go out this way if you like. It's quicker and I'm going to meet Dr Bolton in the staff room.'

'Oh,' she stopped. 'Is he...?'

'No, our staff room is on the first floor.'

As he let her pass into the narrow corridor, Colin appeared on the stairs.

'Marsha,' he called, dashing halfway down until he was able to lean over the bannister, his head above hers. 'What kind of shirt did Christine wear?'

'Leave me alone!' she shouted, cringing back against the wall.

'Get off her back, mate!' George warned.

'Sorry, I really need to know!'

'Get away from her. Colin, I'll see you upstairs! Go!'

'The shirt! What was the shirt? What was the shirt?' He leapt down the remaining stairs and swung round the newel post, landing between the pair.

'What was the shirt? I've got to know!'

'Go away!' she cried.

In one swift moment, Colin had Marsha pinned against the wall, one hand around her throat. His face pressed so close to hers that she could smell the reek of stale coffee on his breath.

'Let go!' she rasped out hoarsely.

'The shirt!' he hissed.

Marsha glared at him, and he released his grip.

'A cowboy shirt.'

'For Christ's sake! What's got into you?' George pushed Colin away, forcing him to stumble.

'Get out of my sight! I can't believe you've just assaulted a patient!'

By now, Marsha was in tears. 'Get the police! Get the police!' she wailed.

'We'll do that in a moment, when we've all calmed down. Let's go back into the consulting room for a minute.'

George settled Martha on the couch.

'It wasn't real,' she said. 'The shirt wasn't real and Christine wasn't real. You believe me, don't you?'

'Of course I do, there's no problem. But I suggest we meet again next week, just in case this incident has caused any further problems.'

Colin opened the door. He stood there, dishevelled and red. 'She was real... is real! I've seen her.'

George hoisted him by his arms, marched him down the corridor, and physically threw him out of the clinic.

'I'm having you struck off. You'll never work again. If you come within fifty yards of my practice or patients, I'll lay criminal charges. Get away from here!'

Colin ran for his bike and raced down the middle of the road as car horns were sounded from one end to the other.

When he got back home, he threw his bike down on the pavement and barged into the house. He knew his door would be open before he even saw the tell-tale shadow on the wall. There she was: on his sofa, doubled up with laughter. His vision? His hallucination? His Christine? But could the result of an imbalance of neurotransmitters be physically tangible?

He lurched at her. Although her small neck felt solid in his palms and her throat resisted his thumbs, she obstinately refused to dissolve into the nothingness he so desperately wanted.

*****

The following season, Man U did as badly as predicted, but Chelsea did even worse. Mourinho lost his job as Chelsea's manager, and Leicester walked off with the League Cup. Yes, that's right. Leicester City!

*****

In most English pubs, football matches can be watched on huge TV screens. It's amazing how they have become so cheap so rapidly. That's progress for you. They can also be found in hospitals, care homes, and prisons (including high security ones) so murderers and rapists can still watch their favourite teams play on Saturday afternoons.

In Colin's high security unit, patients are only allowed out of their rooms when they can be trusted. As Colin finds it easy to get on with people, he spends most of his time socialising and helping out. He even cleans his own room. Not many inmates do that. Although the domestic staff are excellent, some of the patients get a sense of independence from looking after themselves, and this is encouraged as much as possible. On the occasions when agency workers are used to cover staff absences, Colin has to tell them not to go into his room. However, there have been times when he has found someone, usually someone new to the ward, sitting on his bed. As the doctors know, this can cause stress in a patient, but these rare incidents are usually quickly resolved.

Colin has been a model patient. The staff might say he was their favourite patient: perhaps because of his love of football or maybe because of his extensive knowledge of psychiatry, although he doesn't talk much about that.

'What did you think about the Arsenal's chances after the Chelsea match last night?' said an old lag, who had just come back from lunch. 'Wasn't that goal...?'

'Don't tell me the result,' said Colin quickly, as he walked past. 'I'm watching the replay this afternoon.'

Enthusiasm for football had greatly increased since Colin's arrival and had been a positive influence throughout the hospital. It had been said many times that they all had good reason to be grateful to Colin.

'Who's playing then?' called out a nurse cheerfully.

'Chelsea and Wolves, but don't tell me the result. I want to see the whole match.'

She smiled, putting a folded sheet into a cupboard. She had no interest in football, but it was all useful banter, especially with Colin. He hurried along the corridors. Having made it through lunch without anyone telling him the final score, all he had to do was get to his room.

It was always unlocked. The doors could only be locked from the outside, and these days, that rarely happened. A new more liberal system was being tested. Most of the time, the doors were left wide open to let in the light and air. The wards all had narrow windows, but they were high up. Colin intended to shut his door and watch the match in the low light from above.

A patient, whom Colin had got to know well, called to him from the room opposite. Colin paused at the threshold.

'Hey, Colin, how do you think Chelsea will do?'

'They lose,' said Christine.

4. NURSE JANE

Had you been acquainted with me as a boy, you would have known that my limp had been caused by a careless midwife and that I had very nearly died as a result. I was reliably informed that the culprit was dealt with expediently and never given the chance to injure another newborn, which pleased me somewhat.

Once I had learned the cause of my crooked leg, it became the one thing that defined my childhood. My outbursts of anger were excused, I was exempt from playing rough sports at school, and I was given special dispensation in exams. Chairs were adapted to accommodate the unevenness in my hips, for I was quick to point out that being in one position for any length of time caused an intensity of pain that no one else could imagine.

The condition could have been corrected in my mid-teens, had I not suffered an antipathy towards hospitals nor, indeed, towards anything medical. No amount of endorsement from friends, well-meaning relatives, or optimistic doctors could persuade me to have it treated. If, at first, this was childish attention-seeking behaviour, then it certainly developed very quickly into something that could almost have been called a phobia.

Although I admit to having exaggerated aspects of my infirmity over the years, the antipathy I felt towards hospitals was as real as my limp. I wonder if it may have been due to the knowledge that my birth had been carried out carelessly, so carelessly that the midwife had been summarily dismissed; at least as I thought then. I was assured that if she had not been sacked, my parents could have taken legal proceedings against her as well as against the hospital. My earliest memories, therefore, are of being an object of pity, which later metamorphosed into the self-pity I carried into adulthood.

It was no secret. I would regale any passer-by with my medical history, and, if keen to learn about how life could so randomly throw misfortune at the undeserving, they would continue with the acquaintance. How I eventually became engaged is credit only to the long-suffering patience of my girlfriend, along with the development of a new medical process that someone with my condition could benefit from later in life.

It was only after my engagement that I agreed to undergo the surgery. I cannot blame her for insisting that I should have a steady gait when the time came to walk down the aisle, and she made it a condition for our wedding. Since a cure was possible, she argued, I should pursue it.

Thus it was that my fiancée drove us to Newtown Hospital for what was meant to be my miracle treatment. I had never even had so much as a tetanus injection in my youth, and going to the dentist was a cause of major trauma to me, so when the dreaded day of my hospital appointment arrived, I needed every ounce of inducement and threat that our relationship could take to get into the car, and yet more to get out of it. (Why are so many hospitals designed with façades that are similar in style to those of churches? I am not a churchgoer.) I stumbled behind my girlfriend, using my constant truculence to disguise the worst of my terror. She ignored me until we reached the entrance.

'You're trembling,' she said as we walked through the door. She gently took hold of my arm and guided me to a chair in the circular reception area, while she asked the receptionist for directions. My nervous state was exacerbated by the knowledge that this was the very hospital where I had only just survived birth. Sitting there, feeling so achingly alone, I found the smells and the noise stifling. I looked down at the horribly smooth floor to steady myself.

All too soon, I was up again, and we made our way along a light-blue corridor. We followed the signs that purported to lead to the orthopaedic department, but somehow we ended up in one of the wards. As we stood there uncertainly, a grey figure came gliding up in front of us. No, that is not quite true. Her uniform was blue, but hair and face were grey.

'Are you lost?' she asked in a wistful, far-away voice.

My fiancée stated our destination, and the nurse pointed back the way we had come. I groaned.

'Just go straight to the stairs, then take the passage opposite, and it's at the end. You'll see it. It won't do you any good here, this is part of the maternity wing.'

'Maternity,' I repeated ominously.

'This area,' she continued, making a show with her hands, 'is exactly as it has been since the war. That's why the directions aren't as clear as they should be. The rest of it is all new.'

'And improved?' I spoke sardonically. Oh, was I ready to be critical!

'I'm the matron in charge of this department. Are you here for treatment?'

'I'm having surgery to correct the effects of medical incompetence.'

'I am sorry to hear that.'

'Let's see if they actually get it right this time.'

'I'm sure they will. Maybe I'll pop in to see you on the orthopaedic ward later.'

'If they don't kill me first.'

'Come on,' said my ever-patient love.

But I was warming to my narrative. 'This is the mess they made of me last time I was here,' I said, limping a few demonstrative steps.

'Thank you for your help, matron,' said my fiancée firmly.

The matron glanced at a clock above us, and then hurried off through an archway near a barely visible exit sign. I glanced through it, but she was nowhere to be seen. We retraced our steps back to the stairs.

'I cannot understand how anyone knows where they're meant to be in this place,' I said. 'That's probably why they don't know what they're doing.'

A nurse on the stairs turned to look at us, before continuing her ascent without another glance.

'She probably heard you,' my fiancée whispered.

'Good!'

'This is what you always do,' she chided. 'You drive people away all the time.'

When we finally reached the orthopaedic department, I was unpleasantly rushed into a gown and onto a trolley. My heart was racing, and I was sweating. My fiancée had left for the waiting room as soon as she had seen me sign the consent form. The sedative followed, and, was it my imagination, or did that needle look large enough to pierce the hide of an elephant? If they had given me a little more time, perhaps I would not have been so stressed. If they had just taken everything at a reasonable pace or explained things more clearly, I would have been fine, but I was shaking and panicking right from the start.

No. I had decided: it was not to be. I could live with my slight disfigurement if necessary, and if that was to be the end of my engagement, then so be it. I sat up on the trolley and waved my hand with as much finality as I could muster. They tried to push me back down, but I slipped from their grasp with a deftness that surprised even me.

'That's it!' I said, as I stood on the floor, 'I've changed my mind. I'm discharging myself.' And I strode towards the archway, making for the brightly-lit exit sign with a feeling that was more than relief: it was exhilaration.

'Hold on!' A nurse darted in front of me, blocking my way. 'If you go through there, you can't come back.'

'I don't care,' I answered.

'I care. Don't leave.'

'But it's up to me what I do.'

'It is,' she said. 'In the final analysis, it is. But you're a big boy now. Consider this: it is only a simple routine operation, and if you go through with it, you have a chance of a really good outcome and a really good life.'

'I've made my decision.'

She tried to bar my way, but I was so angry I pushed past her.

'Maybe next year,' I said as I entered the archway.

'There will *be* no next year!' she shouted after me. She seemed just as angry as I. More so, in fact. 'If you walk out of here, you won't get treated in this hospital or anywhere, for that matter!'

Heads turned towards me, and my indignation was as inflamed as my anger. It was about time she learnt some facts. I turned and faced her again.

'Let me tell you something,' I shouted back. 'It's all because of you that I'm here! If it wasn't for some useless midwife...'

'Yes, yes.' she sneered. 'The same old story. I know all the facts about your birth and the fuss that was made. You've made the most of that, haven't you? Poor you! One small mistake that anyone could have made.'

'Small mistake?' I said. 'Well, just look at me now!' I performed my exaggerated walk.

'You deserve an Oscar,' she said.

'How dare you!' I bellowed. 'I nearly died! My heart stopped. I've have had to endure the consequences of that for a whole lifetime. That useless nurse hasn't!'

The air stilled for a moment and hung heavily.

'Oh, but she has, and for much longer,' the nurse said quietly.

Everyone was looking at me as if it were my fault that some stupid midwife had been sacked because of her own ineptitude.

Someone called out, 'You selfish little man! How is your fiancée going to feel?'

I was about to reply, but whoever it was had vanished, and I paused, hesitating. Actually, he was right. I did care what she thought. I knew what she would think of me if I walked out of that hospital. As I thought of my fiancée, my self-control returned. I glanced at the nurse. Her expression had changed.

'You need to learn to earn respect,' she said, 'and not play the sympathy card all the time.'

I looked at the glowing exit sign and then at the darkness where I had been lying. I did not think they would want to operate on me now.

'What do I do now?' I said miserably.

'You don't have to leave,' she said. 'I can help you back.'

I allowed the nurse to lead me back to the trolley, and she tried to help me onto it.

'Let me be,' I said irritably. 'I can do it.' I clambered up and lay down flat.

'Good,' she said. 'Just so you know, I'm Nurse Jane.'

I huffed testily to try and disguise my returning fear.

'Turn your face the other way and you won't see anything.'

I faced the wall and she slowly leant over me. I could see her earrings hanging down close to my face.

'Count backwards from ten,' she said.

'Why are you wearing such long earrings?' I said, stifling my terror with false bravado.

'Count down,' she said briskly.

'Long earrings,' I repeated, and that is all I remember.

*****

A moment later, I woke up feeling fuzzy-headed and nauseous. At least, I thought it was only a moment later, but anaesthetised sleep does not provide any sense of the passage of time. When waking from normal sleep, one may have a good idea of the number of hours that have passed. In the morning, I can usually guess the time to the nearest half hour, even without the help of daylight leaking through the curtain. However, coming round from an operation is different: it seems as though no more than a few moments have passed since the anaesthetist's needle was inserted into the vein. My first thoughts were that I was still awaiting the sedative. Something was clamped hard against my face. I pushed it away and saw steam. It was an oxygen mask.

'Oh, good,' a gentle female voice coaxed me out of the oblivion. 'You're awake. Just keep that on a bit longer till the doctor comes round.'

I retched and squeezed my dry lips into shapes, eventually making some sort of sound.

The nurse understood me. 'It's all done. It's all over,' she said.

I sucked in the oxygen more deeply. The fuzziness subsided and I began to see more clearly. There was a drip in my wrist and another line going under the covers. I did not remember being told anything about drips and oxygen masks.

My fiancée was supposed to take me home that afternoon. I tried to say her name, but I was unable to make the right sound. I felt a growing discomfort that might have been terror had I had been completely sensible. The nurse was still there, adjusting the various paraphernalia.

'She's just gone home, your fiancée. You missed her by a few minutes. Don't worry, I'll phone her and tell her you're awake. She said she'd come straight back.'

'Gone home?' She was supposed to wait for me in the hospital. 'Am I in intensive care?' I asked, suspiciously.

'No,' she chuckled reassuringly. 'This is the close monitoring room, but we'll be moving you to one of the recovery wards shortly.' She took a clipboard from the end of the bed. 'The procedure itself went very well, but the doctor will tell you why we're keeping an eye on you for a while.'

I dozed off again, only to be woken after a short period by the doctor himself. He removed the oxygen mask and the lines. Two nurses unhitched the bed from the wall and I was wheeled away with the doctor walking behind. As we went out into the light-blue corridor, he caught up with us and explained what had happened. The operation had been a success, and I could expect to walk properly, but there had a little problem during the operation. It seems I had momentarily flatlined.

'It's not as serious as it sounds,' he reassured me. 'It's just one of those things that can happen in any operation, albeit rarely these days.'

'How did it happen?' I asked.

The doctor looked squarely at me. 'Your blood pressure dropped suddenly. We don't exactly know why. As I said, these things can happen. But there were plenty of us on standby to start you up again.'

'So my heart actually stopped? Like it did when I was born?'

'Only for a very short time. There was no damage. Fortunately, it happened at the end just as we'd finished all the work.'

I thought about this. For the second time in my life, my heart had stopped. I should have been shocked, or even terrified, but I noticed that I wasn't even worried.

The doctor continued. 'We had to put you in an induced coma to make sure there were no underlying problems that might have caused it. We also needed to give your heart a good chance to get back into its regular pattern.'

'How long was I out for?'

'Three days.'

'So what day is it?'

'Sunday the seventh.'

That is the nature of comas. One has no sense of how long one has been dead to the world.

'So am I all right now?'

'All your signs are good, but I'd like to see you stand before I go. Nurse Sarah will help you.'

Nurse Sarah. I tried to remember the names of the other nurses I had met.

Nurse Sarah held my hands as I twisted round and put both feet flat on the floor. Supported by her, I stood up and tentatively put one foot in front of the other. For the first time in my life, I could feel all my toes spread themselves evenly on the hard floor. It was wonderful! I would like to say it was like being born again, but as I am not a god-fearing man, I feel uncomfortable making such a comparison.

'Oh my, look at you!' sang the nurse.

My first few steps proved that the operation had been successful, and the doctor clapped encouragingly. I may not believe in the supernatural, but I noticed there were tears in my eyes as I walked a few more steps. I had soon done enough to prove to myself and everyone else that I could walk normally.

From now on, my life was going to be very different. I was going to stop playing on people's sympathy. Something jerked into my memory: a vague recollection of someone talking about earning respect.

'You'll certainly be going home today, as planned,' said the doctor.

I sat down on the bed. And then it came to me: I remembered who had given me that advice. I also recalled the tantrum I had thrown before the operation, so my next feeling was one of embarrassment.

'I should apologise,' I said, 'for the trouble I caused before I had my sedative.'

'Trouble?' said the doctor.

'You know,' I said. 'Nearly walking out on my operation like that.'

'I didn't know you did,' he said.

'You weren't there,' I answered.

'When you had your anaesthetic? Yes, I was. I was supervising.'

A passing nurse wrinkled her brow haughtily in stark contrast to my humility. Then the grey figure of the matron wafted into the ward and joined in the conversation.

'Anyway,' I persisted, 'I really have to apologise to Nurse Jane. I remember she had long earrings. She talked some sense into me.'

'We don't wear earrings in the hospital,' said the matron. 'Jewellery has been banned for years, hasn't it, doctor?'

'It has.'

I did not understand. I could recall those earrings very clearly. 'I can tell you Nurse Jane was certainly wearing a pair,' I said. 'They were quite nice, as it happens.'

The matron folded her arms authoritatively. 'As for any Nurse Jane,' she said dismissively, 'the only Nurse Jane I know was only here for a short time. She was a midwife. She wore long earrings, but she's been dead for many years.'

5. THE 6TH MOMENT OF THE RIEMANN ZETA FUNCTION

As he scanned the rows of figures and formulae, Archie Pellgrave wished he hadn't quit smoking. They were set out before him on the thin tissue paper that MI6 delivered in such abundance when they didn't want to send data over the internet. Binomials: he wasn't even sure he could remember what they were. Since working his way up from humble maths graduate to management, the world of calculus had become a distant memory, along with cheap beer and rag balls. He had enjoyed many promotions, some formal, some more discreet; but that's the way it happens in the service. This latest problem had come from an Exeter University research project, which had been referred up to him by people with long memories. Fortunately, Lance Mulligan was the man in Exeter, and he would know what a binomial was. Archie put his hand to his mouth and found a cigarette wasn't there.

*****

There had been some talk of building a theatre in the city and redeveloping the dreadful area around the bus station. Nothing would be better than to get rid of the derelict shops and condemned flats that had been built after the Blitz. The devastation caused by explosive objects suddenly dropping from the sky gave the low-end builders, second-rate town planners, and other patriots the opportunity to make a quick fortune, while Germany carefully restored cities like Dresden to their former glory.

Unfortunately, it was not to be. The council's finance department couldn't (or wouldn't) ratify the rebuild, so the big shows continued to go to Plymouth while the people of Exeter contented themselves with the smaller theatres, such as the one on the university campus. It was a good space in many respects, but (aside from being located up a steep hill and hard to find) parking was a nightmare. Should a theatre-goer eventually find the right car park, there was no guarantee they would be able to park in it. And if they were fortunate enough to be in the right place at the right time, they would invariably get lost finding their way to the venue.

Complaints were regularly made. These complaints turned into moans, and, like gravity, moans travel downwards. At Exeter University, they went spiralling down through middle management, down to the very depths of lower management, and down again until they reached the desk of Eric Scufton, dogsbody extraordinaire.

'I mean, really Eric… that camper van, if you can call it that, has been there all week and probably longer. It's your job to…'

So at six o'clock under a low autumnal sky, with the proverbial flea firmly ensconced in his ear, Eric stomped to Car Park C. Sure enough, there was the van. The stomps, decreasing in stride length while increasing in intensity, took him to the side of the van, against which he banged and hallooed admirably. Nothing happened. He waited, and repeated the exercise again with the same result. So the proverbial flea did the proverbial flea equivalent of sticking its feet up in front of the telly and opening a beer. Eric yelled something obscene, kicked the door, waved his arms into determined X and Y shapes, and then started hitting the windscreen.

'Whu… yeah?' The divider between the driving seat and sleeping quarters slid apart, and a bleary face appeared.

'No overnight camping. Can't you read or are you stupid?'

Kevin Saunders, MA Oxon, soon to be PhD, made a show of looking out of the side window at the indicated notice.

'Uhh, yeah.'

Dressed in purple pyjamas, he clambered over the seat and started the engine. A sudden "yip yip" emanated from a little terrier as surprised as Kevin to find itself in motion so soon after settling down for a sleep. The van inched reluctantly out of a space reserved for lecturers and their guests.

'And don't come back!'

Kevin drove slowly through the campus and into town, where he negotiated a large roundabout and selected the road to Exmouth.

*****

As Lance was checking the computer security of an upcoming firm on behalf of their auditors, to which he had been seconded, there was a high-pitched whine on his phone. He looked at the screen. There he found the figures sent by Archie Pellgrave. The state of being seconded was symbiotic: Lance got to see into systems to which he would otherwise have had no legitimate access, and the customer got the best possible forensic checks that existed outside Germany. There was also the added incentive of a lucrative financial stream, which, these days, cannot be ignored by any government department, no matter how important they believe themselves to be.

'Got it, sir,' he said into his mobile phone. 'It's the Riemann zeta function. I know it well. It's the closest anyone's got to finding a pattern in the occurrence of prime numbers.'

'You were very quick with that one, Lance. I'm impressed!' said Archie.

'So what's the deal with it? Someone's got the 6th moment, have they? When did they get the 4th? 1960s?'

'No, they haven't, and it wouldn't be a problem for us if they had. Incidentally, it was worked out to its 4th order of 10 back in 1926.'

'Wheoo. You'd think with all these computers that we could handle logarithmic functions somewhere down the line. They must be close to the 6th, but it would be good if we got there first, for once.'

'The Chinese will probably get there first, simply due to the sheer number of data inputters and single-mindedness. Unless, of course, we get a smart arse. Smart arses trump attrition every time, and that's when you get the paradigm shift. But that's not what they're worried about. There's a bit more to it: the Dutch are on to something.'

'Can you tell me?'

'Not yet. We're monitoring developments there, but I need you to land someone for me.'

'Not Protocol 19?' Lance could not disguise his unease. As the man on the ground, Protocol 19 was one of the things that would automatically fall to him. Nobody liked it, and he had recently had a horrible experience with it.

'No, no, we aren't anywhere near that stage. It's only a university lecturer. I just want you to sound him out, that's all. Should be a quick job. Then come straight back to London... Oh, and bring some ciggies.'

*****

Kevin had intended to drive to Exmouth, where there was an abandoned college at the top of a hill. The road alongside it invited overnight parking, and there were always several other camper vans lined up, providing safety in numbers. Shortly after leaving the city limits, he passed a pink building with a large car park that was almost full. It was the Bridge Inn: an old pub that originally would have been lime-washed with hog's blood for waterproofing, now it was merely painted pink. His students had told him about it.

He cautiously steered off the main road and parked on some grass at the far end. As he changed into a woolly top and jeans, he considered his chances of staying overnight. There was also the risk of meeting his students, which he tried to avoid when off-duty (and occasionally when on-duty), but he suspected they wouldn't stray this far from campus on such a cold weekday evening. This convinced him, and he made up his mind to go in for a drink. Picking up his scraggle of a terrier, he put it on its lead and walked alongside the river towards the building. A man came out of the door.

'Hi,' he called. 'Am I allowed to bring my dog in, d'you think?'

'Have you been here before?'

'No.'

The man laughed. 'You can do anything you like, but don't let the landlady catch you on your mobile phone!'

'I haven't got a mobile phone.'

'You're all right then.' And he held the door open for Kevin and his dog.

There was no bar as such. Instead, customers purchased beer from a taproom situated off a dark wood-panelled corridor. Kevin made his way along it and bought a half of something hoppy. He stepped into the farther of the two drinking areas, a snug, but it was nearly full, so he retreated. It had a small serving hatch through which Kevin could see several people sitting in the taproom itself. He wandered into the empty lounge, where dogs were welcome, and spent the next hour sipping his beer.

As he was contemplating his next course of action, Lance looked in and saw Kevin sitting there alone.

'Nice van,' he said. 'Yours?'

The van predated tracking devices, but it hadn't taken long for the traffic cameras to pick up his number plate and to work out that it was heading towards Topsham. It had taken even less intuition and time to spot it in the pub grounds.

'It does for me,' said Kevin. 'I live in it. I've just been caught sleeping on Exeter Uni's campus, so I'll have to find somewhere else for the night.'

'Camping on campus,' said Lance. 'Good for you!' And he shook his hand. He liked a talkative fellow.

'Well, I work there,' said Kevin. 'I'm researching number theory, so I do a bit of lecturing too. Here.' He gave him a card.

'Oxford,' commented Lance.

'Fifteen years ago. After that, I sort of dropped out. They called me back later to do a PhD and Exeter seemed like a good base.'

'And number theory?'

'It's supposed to be a bit hush-hush, but it's well known that the spread of zeros in the error margin for the Riemann zeta function just about corresponds with the Eigenvalues that describe atomic vectors.'

Lance drained his half-pint glass, and Kevin supped his last drop.

'I'm afraid I can't stay long, I've got the dog to see to.'

'Let me get you one more. I love science. Stay there.'

While Lance went for refills, other drinkers came into the lounge and asked him about his dog. The dog seemed to realise this and enthusiastically pricked up its ears. It sat with its mouth half-open as if it were smiling, just as the landlady walked in.

'Oh, look at you,' she said appreciatively. 'You know, we'll have to get another dog for the Bridge.'

'That would be nice,' said Kevin, 'especially here.'

'It would. Next year for definite. Come what may, I'm getting a dog!'

As she left, Lance returned and put the beers in front of them.

'I got pints,' he said. 'You can have the darker one. Is that all right?'

It was. Kevin had never tasted anything as delicious as that West Country ale, served straight from the barrel in the stone cellar. This is how beer was always meant to be served, not pumped through dirty pipes into even dirtier glasses.

'If you put in some really big numbers, you get more Eigenvalues,' said Kevin. 'There is a school of thought that says we might come up with patterns that correspond to the periodic table. I've got a friend at Delft who thinks he's nearly proved it.'

'Delft? Isn't that the big university in Holland?'

'Yeah. I've been sending some of my stuff to help him. Money is a bit tight there, as it is over here, but I heard today that he's got a massive grant. It's quite exciting! The first results seem to correspond with the elements we know, and so, by implication, we can find out more about the ones we don't by scaling up. Theoretically, we could predict the atomic numbers of elements with half-lives that are so short we'd never be able to observe them, not even with the Hadron.'

Kevin finished his pint, and once more Lance headed out of the room with the empty glasses. But instead of going straight to the taproom, he nipped out through the front door and phoned Archie.

'He's sending data to someone in Holland,' he said.

'That explains the Dutch interest. The problem is that this stuff's not covered by the Official Secrets Act, so it's never been on anyone's radar.'

'So, can't we just tell him not to do it?'

'We need to make sure the Chinese aren't involved,' said Archie. 'There are a lot of Chinese students at Exeter. I need you to get into the central systems to find out who, what, and how much anyone knows.'

'If you can sort me out a cover, I'll go in early tomorrow.'

'Right-o. I'll send you an SP1. By the way, when you report back, don't forget my fags.'

'You know what I'm going to say.'

'I know, I know. I promised the missus I wouldn't buy anymore.'

'I'll keep the phone on,' said Lance. 'I'll see if I can pump some more out of him.'

The pub also served beer in third-of-a-pint glasses, so Lance choose four different ones to sample. He pushed the strongest towards Kevin.

'This'll be my last,' said Kevin. 'I'm in early tomorrow.'

'Not as early as me,' thought Lance, putting the phone on the bench beside him so Archie could listen in.

The conversation continued, and when Kevin cited the logarithm for dealing with the higher numbers, Lance thought he heard Archie gasp. By the time Kevin had got up to take the dog outside, he had finished two of the drinks to Lance's one. He picked up the phone again, but Archie had rung off, so he called him back.

'Paradigm shifts and smart arses,' said Archie. 'We've woken up Area Three to check out his stuff and boy, are they worried! If he's on the ball, and the Chinese have got their hands on it, they'll be able to make nuclear bombs out of duck feathers!'

'Hold on, he's coming back.'

'Keep the line open.'

'Sorry,' said Kevin, as he breezed in and picked up the last beer. 'He needed a little walk.'

'What about your research team, are they all doing PhDs?'

'One of them is. Two are technically retired, and then there's Simon.' He rubbed his chin.

'Simon?'

'Simon Ling. I don't quite know what he's doing. He is very interesting though. He does some lecturing too, like me.'

'Well,' said Lance calmly, 'he's probably from a Chinese University.'

'Yeah, maybe.' He smacked his lips and held the glass up to the light. 'I reckon this is the best one of them all.'

'Another?'

'I shouldn't really… Oh, go on then.'

'Yip!' barked the terrier.

*****

That night, Kevin slept comfortably in his van while Lance curled up awkwardly in his car, which he had parked in the grounds of a farm shop further up the road. Archie phoned just after midnight.

'We've been onto this Simon Ling, and he doesn't check out. I've called Washington. Make sure you're in early tomorrow and get everything.'

'Perhaps I will if you let me sleep this side of midnight!'

*****

Lance was as good as his word. As soon as the SP1 came through, he walked into the maths building and flashed his ID card at the weary receptionist who hardly glanced at it.

'The computer man!' she yelled up the stairs. Taking that as a direction, he went straight to the upper floor and found a new computer suite. He logged onto the nearest PC and quickly cracked the firewalls. HR records, research data, and email accounts opened up to him like a suicidal spatchcock chicken. When two students walked in, he turned his face away and continued his work. They sat with their backs toward him, totally uninterested. One of them opened a can of drink.

'I've come in for nothing today,' he said. 'Ling's absent.'

The other student grunted in sympathy and opened a bag of crisps, which they shared. Soon the whole room smelt of crisps and students.

After Lance had sucked the databases dry, he went back downstairs. The receptionist greeted him with a yawn.

'Where's Mr Ling?' he asked.

She rubbed her eyes and swallowed hard. 'He's gone to visit a sick aunt in Bradford,' she said. 'Apparently.'

As Kevin pulled into Car Park C, he passed Eric who scratched his head when he saw him. He stomped after the van and waited angrily while he parked.

'I thought I told you to get lost!' he said.

'I work here,' said Kevin. 'I'm in the research department.'

The proverbial flea was proverbially joyous. Eric turned to stomp towards the staff canteen and nearly knocked Lance over.

'I say,' said Kevin, 'it's you, isn't it? Thanks for the beers last night. Are you part of the uni? You never told me.'

'No. I just do the computers. Your Simon Ling fellow is off again. That must be irritating for you.'

'Is he? That's strange. He's always been really reliable. I wonder what's up.'

'I heard it was another sick aunt,' said Lance getting into his car.

'You lot are all the same,' jeered Eric. 'Sick aunts? Workshy more like.' And he went off to annoy the canteen staff.

Lance got into his car and drove off. He had all the information he needed. He parked in Exeter, walked to the station, and took the train to Paddington. Archie pushed the proffered cigarettes away.

'I've given up for good,' he said. 'You can keep them.'

The packet stayed on the table while they went through the recently retrieved data.

'No porn,' said Lance.

'Shame,' said Archie. 'The Riemann zeta conundrum has moved on overnight. I'd say it's at an advanced stage now. I'll put this straight through to Washington now, and they'll have to shut it down. It's all turning rather nasty.'

'What about Ling?'

'Not a trace. The feds were all ready to bring down a flight if they could prove he was on it. They're all over the place at the moment.'

Lance was horrified.

'It's been done before,' said Archie calmly. 'Look, even we're not supposed to know this, and it's never been completely confirmed, but remember that 9/11 plane that the passengers were supposed to have brought down? Well, they didn't. The black box recordings were doctored to make it seem like they did. Homeland Security brought it down. Anyway, it seems that we're now on amber alert, so we have to find Ling double-quick.'

'And Saunders?'

'They're still trying to pull him in. He left the university at lunchtime.'

'Softly-softly, I would suggest,' said Lance.

'It's not up to me anymore, but I just wondered... unofficially... if you could go back undercover and get to him first? It might slow things down a bit.'

'I'll email him and suggest we meet in the pub for an early drink.'

*****

Eric and his amazing dancing flea ejected Kevin from the campus as soon as the morning session finished, so he had to drive all the way back to Exmouth to find a parking space where he wouldn't be disturbed. The road outside the old college was choc-a-bloc, but there was no one was working on-site. He forced open the gate and parked behind a disused church, where the bushes growing out of its side obscured his van.

He opened his laptop and settled down to look at the formulae again. There had to be an error in there somewhere; he just couldn't get it to work on the larger numbers. He closed his eyes, took a deep breath, and opened them again. Tapping at the keys, he turned the formula into a Hermitian matrix and started all over again.

His dog was getting restless, so he decided to take a break and walk around the church. As it stopped to fertilize a tree root, he looked in through the window of the church. Expecting an altar or a font, he was surprised to see beer pumps arranged along a bar. Suddenly, a drink seemed like a good idea.

As he drove back to the Bridge Inn, his registration number was picked up by various traffic cameras and the data sent straight to MI6. Kevin parked up and, leaving his dog in the van, just had the one beer he'd promised to himself. Arriving back at Exeter station, Lance picked up his car, made an intelligent guess based on the last known sighting, and drove to Topsham. He parked in a cul-de-sac by a mini roundabout on the brow of a hill and walked down to the Bridge. It had started to rain and by the time he walked through the door, just ten minutes after Kevin had left, he was soaked through. He ordered a half of Branoc. The lounge was empty, so he sat in the snug, where a large woodstove burned and a lively conversation was underway.

'Hi,' said a bald fellow in a scruffy top.

'Hi,' said Lance, taking it as an invitation to sit at the same table.

A man in army fatigues who was sitting by the woodstove commented on the steam rising from his wet clothes.

'So,' said the scruffy man, by way of continuing the conversation, 'a Hermitian matrix is made up of complex numbers, each with a real part and an imaginary part equal in value but opposite in sign. That's what he meant.'

'That's what who meant?' asked Lance.

'This mathematician fellow. He's proving a theory. I got him to write it all down for me.'

The man by the fire laughed. 'It's amazing who you meet in the Bridge.'

'Are you a mathematician?' asked Lance.

The scruffy man laughed. 'No. I never bothered. I'm a musician, a harpist. Here's my CD. Go on... take it. It's free.'

Lance took the disc. 'I'm more interested in that formula,' he said. 'Can you show me what he wrote?'

The musician took out two screwed-up pieces of A4 and spread them on the table. Lance took out his phone and photographed them. He sent them straight to Archie.

'I hope they're not copyright,' said the man by the fire.

'If they belong to anyone, they belong to him, and he didn't seem to care about letting me have them,' replied the harpist. 'By the way, have I given you my CD?

Lance's phone buzzed.

'Sorry lads,' he said, and went into the corridor to take the call.

Every phone within a half-mile radius suddenly went dead, with the exception of his line of communication with Archie.

'That's it! That's exactly it!' said Archie. 'You've given me the complete formula. Washington's in turmoil. One of our subs is in the Bohai Sea with its Tridents primed. Hold on, I need a fag.'

'What?' Lance heard Archie's lighter click.

'Pre-emptive.' Archie sucked on his cigarette. 'We're taking out their entire capability in one go.'

'Wait a minute...' said Lance.

'It'll be a limited strike. Unless Russia deploys.'

'How limited? A nuclear strike?'

'Hold it, Lance, something's come through. Russia is on the move. There's trouble. Their subs have been detected. Washington thinks they've had the same idea.' Archie spoke coolly.

'What sort of idea?' whispered Lance.

'Pre-emptive strikes, Lance. Your nearest bunker is under an old asylum in Sowton. This is the code, I'll say it only once...'

The musician poked his head round the door and called out to him. 'It doesn't work, you know. He told us he'd found that out this afternoon, so don't worry about copyright!'

But Lance was too busy memorising the code to take notice of what he was saying.

A woman came out of the serving area and shook a box in front of him. 'That's fifty pence,' she said. 'We don't use mobile phones in the Bridge.'

*****

Wisps of smoke rose from a lorry lay-by on the road to Budleigh Salterton. A passing police car stopped and reversed into it. As soon as Kevin saw it approach, he poured water on the small fire he had made from the least damp twigs and leaves he had found by the hedgerow. Constable Warbouys exited his vehicle with a good slam of the door and ambled towards him.

'I don't know what you think you're playing at,' he said, 'but this happens to be a public highway.'

'I know,' said Kevin. 'Sorry, sir. I was just boiling up some soup. I didn't want to use the stove because I'd have to run the engine.'

Warbouys was fond of the outdoors, and, in the right place and well supervised, he liked nothing better than a good bonfire. He also liked being called "sir"; it didn't happen very often these days.

'Yip!' The terrier bounced out of the van and the policeman stroked its ears.

He'd been with the force for forty years and was close to retirement. He would like to spend a lot of his retirement outdoors. Receiving a polite apology from an intelligent man, whose dog had let him stroke it, appeased him.

'Make sure you put it right out, and don't let it happen again. I've clocked your van, so my colleagues will be on the lookout for any more shenanigans, got it?'

'I have, sir. Thanks.'

The van, having been "clocked", was duly pinpointed by a GPS map reference, and Lance had a straight run out from Topsham.

It didn't take long before Washington confirmed that the formula was flawed and tensions de-escalated. The Dutch mathematician had been right, in as far as that strange correlation with the periodic table was only coincident at very few points. This became much clearer when the matrix was turned into a graph. However, because MI6 couldn't rule out further extrapolation, it would have to be "contained". Washington was deadly serious concerning that last point. There could only be one outcome and, to this end, Lance was ordered to carry out the dreaded Protocol 19. This distressed him so much that he planned to hand in his notice as soon as the rotten business was over.

Lance Mulligan saw espionage as a game of intellect and strategy. To him, the taking of human life was a symptom of systematic failure. The closest he had come to a Protocol 19 was when Edward Snowden, after his ethical concerns were ignored, leaked classified information gleaned from his work with the NSA and escaped to Russia. Mulligan was immediately booked on a flight to Moscow under a pseudonym. He had just collected his gun from Contact 17 when the Skripal incident kicked off in Salisbury, and his mission was aborted. The reason he was given was that "we can't be seen doing to the Russkies what they are doing to us".

He drove to the lay-by with his Glock 17 handgun in his jacket pocket. Two lorries were parked there along with the van. He drove past it and parked the car on a verge further up the road. Then he walked quietly back towards the lay-by. The back doors of the van were wide open and the interior was lit. Kevin was surprised to see him.

'You're keen,' he said. 'How did you find me?'

'I have ways,' said Lance.

The researcher laughed. 'I've got some more stuff on that theory,' he said. 'That's if you're still into matrices and curves.'

'I could be.' Kevin turned round, fishing about for something in the back of the van. This gave Lance the opportunity he needed. The best he could do was to make the job as quick and painless as possible. He aimed the muzzle at the point in his back where his heart was located.

There was a shrill whine and he replaced the gun in his pocket.

He pulled out his phone and read the message that accompanied the noise.

"Cancel P19", the text read. "Cat out of bag." He scrolled down. "Harpist turned formula into song. Gone viral." There was more. "L traced to aunt in Bradford. End of message."

Kevin turned back to him holding a couple of little round bowls. 'Soup?' he said.

6. INTRUDERS

ACT I SCENE 1

INTERIOR: KITCHEN. DAY. A WOMAN STANDS AT AN IRONING BOARD IN FRONT OF THE WINDOW. SHE HOLDS AN IRON.

WOMAN

Well, I had just done his shirt collar, and I was still holding the red-hot iron, when it happened. They were right there.

(She breathes out slowly and stands still for a moment) There was no doubt, they had found me. 'Why me?' you might think. Why me? I might think that as well. But no, it wasn't as if I hadn't expected them.

If I cast my mind back over the aberrations of the past few months, I can see that I've taken risks, I've been led on. There's been a lot of emotion, and it's all there for anyone to see. I've got myself into a lot of situations that in my former life I'd never have believed. Never in a million years!

Sometimes, I've had to call for help when it's all got too much, and I've always been given that help. I've got some good people around me, I know that. Otherwise, I wouldn't have taken so many risks.

I don't mind admitting there were times when I felt like giving up and just walking away. I could've done that early on; I can't now. None of us can. That's the way it is with crime, you can't leave it alone. Well, that's what I've found anyway.

I persuaded myself I'd only got into this because I wanted more from life. I felt like I deserved more. And I'll tell you what, I've confronted my worst fears head on, and I've come to know myself better. I know what I'm capable of now. Not everyone can say that about themselves!

Most of the others in the group have come to know me a bit better as well, whether they've liked it or not. It's affected people outside the group too: my family, I mean. Of course, it was bound to.

(She sighs) Look, I didn't really think I'd have intruders here though, not in my own home. Maybe I should've known better than to start all this. Don't get me wrong, I wasn't the worst. There are some women I've come to know well, who, it turned out, were capable of a lot more than me. All you have to do is step out of your comfort zone, and the next thing you know, you're taking those first cautious steps into the unknown.

They ease you into it gently. They give you simple tasks to carry out so they can keep an eye on you. Once you show you can cope with those, they give you harder assignments, and so on. And you're dragged into it before you know it.

Oh, and we talk about what we do quite casually. I just sit there, not commenting. You wouldn't believe the deceit, the illicit affairs, the brazen robberies, and not just bank robberies either. And we all talk about it as if it's everyday banter!

I can tell you, though; I never thought I'd have seen myself in this set of circumstances, not in a million years! Never! I s'pose it could just as easily have happened to the others, but it hasn't. Maybe it's only me they've sneaked into in that stealthy, unexpected way of theirs. We've all laid ourselves open to them, and the implications have been enormous.

(Low) I must keep my voice down. I don't actually know how many intruders are here, but I do know that the first thing to do is to ascertain the danger. I know that from experience. The big question is how. Right, I mustn't move. I must think first because the worst possible outcome may yet arise. Oh, my heart's pounding!

STILL HOLDING THE IRON, SHE RESTS THE END OF IT ON THE EDGE OF THE BOARD.

I really needed to know a bit more before something like this happened. Perhaps I should unplug the iron first.

The first thing I'm thinking about is what would've happened if I hadn't been here, and Chloe had been attacked? She's my daughter. I know that sounds horrible, but you have to consider all the possibilities. What if I'd come back from shopping or something, and there she was with a knife held against her throat?

There are things you can do, even when facing the most extreme adversity. Our leader knows I can deal with some pretty awful situations 'cos I'm good at strategy. Strategies make crime easier. I know how to stab someone too. I know how to do it so they don't make a sound. It's elbow round the mouth, and knife just under the shoulder so they drown. You weren't expecting that from a housewife like me, were you?

Well, I can also tell you, I've done it! Oh yes! We'd gone to this ramshackle cottage, and there was this terrible storm. It was all to do with money, but that's the boring bit.

Blackmail's interesting too. I've tried my hand at that as well, on our leader's advice. If someone's got a big enough secret, they'll pay anything. You mustn't lose your nerve though; I found that out soon enough. If you've got someone desperate enough to pay you a fortune, they'll be desperate enough to do anything else as well. That's how it usually works.

But now, well, I'm completely exposed. You see, ultimately I'll be answerable to our leader, and if I've messed up, well, everyone will know. Some of them will be very happy to see my downfall. I've had a bit too much endorsement lately, despite being the newest to the group. As I say, it's crime, see? You either take to it or you don't.

And as for these intruders, p'raps I should call for help. If I could only find my phone. I'm sure it's here somewhere. Yes, help is always at the end of the phone, but I wonder if our leader might say that I should just stand on my own two feet? Now, she'd deal with them easily enough. But that doesn't help me though. I could get someone else to come to my aid, but then that humiliating question would be asked, "Maybe she isn't up to it after all?"

No! I should just go straight in, go on the attack: that's what Mrs Oats always says. "Don't delay the inevitable". Then, if I get away with it, I might never have to mention my doubts to anyone: not to my husband, not to my daughter, not to any of my family. They'd be much better off not knowing anything about these intruders or about the danger of them coming here in the first place, or the possibility of their returning. And I certainly wouldn't say anything about what might have happened to Chloe!

I just need to act quickly and comprehensively. I don't want them hanging round here when my husband and daughter come home because that would spell disaster. And, well, I wouldn't stand a chance.

This visit must be a serious one because I already know these intruders. I've encountered them before. When they've come, there's always been others around, so they haven't been able to get to me because someone else has muscled in. And I've been very grateful for the assistance. "Phew", I've said afterwards. That's my lack of confidence again. But that was then. Now, I can think more like a criminal. Experience, you see.

So, why have they chosen this particular moment? It was obvious I'd be here at home, as I usually am, except for the meetings, of course. I've been going to those meetings long enough. Maybe this is like a test? You see, it's one thing to talk about your plans in the meetings, but then I need to prove I can hack it on my own.

Some of the others have got much more courage and energy, and I get a tiny bit jealous. I shouldn't, I know, but I've always been quick to compare myself to other people. I think I've always felt inadequate and maybe that's why I wanted a bit more: a bit more than what this life of a housewife has to offer. So that's why I said yes to Mrs Oats when she offered to take me to that first meeting.

(She sighs deeply) So I shouldn't be thinking of giving up before I've even tried. And there's part of me that wants to make the others feel jealous too. We all want to be the top dog at some time or other, so why shouldn't I? Especially in

front of Mrs Oats. Every dog has its day, as they say, and this might be mine.

(Low) I'll keep my voice down now because those intruders are getting closer. I can hardly breathe! *(Pause)* It won't be long now; they mean business. And I feel something's going to happen in this house that might change my life forever.

FADE IN SOUND OF CLOCK TICKING AND WASHING MACHINE SPIN AND DRAIN CYCLE.

That's the clock. Can you hear it? Tick. Tick. Tick. Oh, and there's the washing machine. I'll have to put the next load in soon.

SHE LOOKS AROUND THE KITCHEN.

Maybe this yellow-tiled kitchen with its fitted, brown cupboards will become the scene of something you'll read about in magazines or even books.

Look at me! I'm still holding this blessed iron! It won't be any good to me now, so it's lucky I've finished that shirt.

SHE LETS GO OF THE IRON AND RUBS HER PALM WITH THE OTHER HAND.

See that window over the sink? See how it goes the whole length of the wall? When I do the washing-up, I look out over our front garden and into the road, and I can watch the whole world go by.

Now, see straight opposite? That's the Crawshaw's house: there on the opposite side of the road. You can just about see into their window. It faces south, which means they've got a north-facing back garden. It's much better to have a south-facing one like us though. You can sit out in the warm sunshine for longer. And it's one of the things that makes our house that little bit more expensive.

But don't you go thinking I'm a snob. We don't have a showy lifestyle, and this isn't a very big house. We don't have much in the way of savings, and Richard is still walking in the foothills of his career. So we can only afford a few luxuries: there's the car, the big widescreen TV, and our annual family holiday.

But I do love the garden. And it would be a good place to deal with those intruders. Who knows? Maybe this will mark a change of fortune. You have to know what you're doing when it comes to crime, and I do. Now this lot are going to be tough, I can tell.

SHE LIFTS UP THE IRON AND HOLDS HER HAND NEAR THE BASE.

It's still red hot, even though I've turned it off, so I can't just leave it. This is one of those things that slows you right down.

I was just getting into the swing of things too, when they arrived, which just goes to show that you've got to be ready to drop everything, as our leader always says. They definitely pick their moment!

Still, the more I think about it, the more it seems to me that the garden might be a good place for when things start to get crazy. But can I get there in time? I'll have to go out of the kitchen, into the lobby, unlock the back door, and by then... No! It doesn't bear thinking about!

SHE PLACES THE IRON IN THE SUPPORT AT THE END OF THE IRONING BOARD AND TURNS HER HEAD AWAY AS IF LISTENING.

Did you hear that? Maybe it was nothing. No, it's no good; they're too close. I'll never make it as far as the garden. Oh, there's that cold feeling in my stomach. I always get that.

SHE STANDS ON TIPTOE AND PEERS THROUGH THE WINDOW.

I can see Mrs Crawshaw through her kitchen window. That's her all right. Mrs Crawshaw has no fear of intruders like these. She's one of those women who keeps their head down and just gets on with it. You know the sort. You can bet she wouldn't be involved in crime. There are no clandestine meetings for her! Well, Mr Crawshaw wouldn't stand for it anyway.

My Richard doesn't exactly approve of what I do, but he can't stop me. Then again, would someone like Mrs Crawshaw ever rob a bank? It's certainly something to consider. I did mention the meetings to her once, but she just pursed her lips and said: *(She mimics Mrs Crawshaw)* "if that's the sort of thing that you need in your life, that's all well and good, but you won't catch me going along". She's right though, you won't.

It's not like you need to be evil for this sort of stuff; you just need to be able to set things up and have some kind of line for when it all goes wrong, because it does, all the time. If you can come up with a strategy, then you can find your way out of anything. It's all about planning and having strategies. That's something else our leader says.

SHE TURNS BACK AND LEANS ON THE IRONING BOARD.

I mean, I've never really thought of myself as having criminal tendencies, but when the opportunity arose, I jumped in with the same gung ho attitude as all the other women there. Well, there's everything from espionage to robbery, and all the complications that follow on from crimes that might never have been uncovered, were it not for the ingenuity of a single, unlikely figure. So I've had lots of opportunities. And I've been proud of what I've managed to get away with! No wonder those intruders have come for me!

You know, so far it's been a day just like one from my previous life. I've been shopping, popped into the supermarket, and already got tea ready for my husband and daughter. I know what they like, and I always do my best to please them. But when I started going to those meetings, well, that was it. Suddenly I had other priorities. Don't get me wrong, it doesn't mean I've let my family down. Far from it. I simply carry on as best as I can under the circumstances. Doesn't everyone?

After Mrs Oats had persuaded me to join, I finally understood what I'd been yearning for all my life. It was meeting all those bold women that did it. Suddenly, so much more in life seemed possible. Oh, I was cautious at first. Apparently, everybody is. As I say, everything has consequences, of course it does. That's the first thing you have to learn. But as soon as you see what you could be getting out of it, you end up diving headfirst into the deepest, darkest waters.

My husband found out soon enough. He didn't approve, of course, but that didn't bother me. Should it have? Now don't take that as meaning that I don't love him or that I'm dissatisfied with everything we've built for ourselves. No, it's just that I found out that crime really excites me. And then I discovered that I could actually do it!

The leader tells me I've got great potential, and, quite frankly, I find that thrilling. If it hadn't been for Mrs Oats, I'd never have done or learnt so much about myself, but she's still so much better at it than me, and I know her life has changed because of it.

All in all, Richard has taken it reasonably well. Chloe is embarrassed, to say the least. I suppose she would be; teenagers have such a strong sense of justice, don't they? Whenever I start a discussion on the subject, she looks the other way and speaks in that dry monotone that I know as being no more than a failed attempt to demonstrate disinterest.

So, I've stopped talking to both of them about the meetings. Anyway, it's not like I can tell either of them exactly what goes on; they'd be completely shocked! It's the crime thing, you see. It's hard to explain how quickly it becomes addictive. I'm even considering doing it as a full-time career, and I certainly haven't told them that, either!

And, as for these intruders, well that's what you come to expect in this line. I wonder what would happen if they ever came for Richard. *(She laughs)* He'd have no hope. *(Pause)* They really have only come for me.

SHE LOOKS AROUND THE KITCHEN.

Now, what could I use? You see, if the floor were still slightly wet, then feasibly someone could slip on it. You have to look at the feasibility of every situation. A burglar could be taken by surprise as he walked in, and I could trip him up from behind the door. While he's slipping and sliding around trying to get up, then it might be possible to sort out his companion at the same time.

Now, is there a sharp knife within reach? Yes, there is! But what if there were more than two of them?

How did they get in? I locked the front door when I left, and when I got back, I let myself in with the key, and locked it again. *(Pause)* The garage! Of course! We've got an adjoining garage with a door through to the kitchen, so if the garage door is forced, then intruders can get in. Anyone can get into the house via the garage. That's it!

So, what to do now? What's the best way to deal with this?

Think fast. If I hesitate now, I'll pay the price. That clock's still ticking away. They came at exactly half past four, and now it's... Oh no, they're still here, and I haven't done anything! Richard could come home any moment. If I don't act soon, there's going to be a scene of some sort, I reckon. *(She mimics him)* "What's going on and what on earth do you think you're doing?" But he doesn't realise that these intruders are something to be reckoned with.

What was it they were about? Come on, I ought to know by now. My mind's in a tizzy. There are various scenarios, some are familiar to me and some not, but that was the point of all those meetings. By now, I should be able to deal with the unexpected, you know, turn it to my advantage. That's what Mrs Oats said on the way to the first meeting.

Now is the time to think clearly, to use what I've spent all that time learning and practising.

My phone! I've just remembered: it's upstairs in the bedroom. I could do with it now, but that means leaving the kitchen. I can't do that; it's too late. Oh dear! Panic, panic! Stay where you are, girl. Breathe.

(She tastes the atmosphere with the tip of her tongue) Right. They're still there. I need to think of a plan. I reckon I could see this through quickly and cleanly, but the clock's still ticking and I haven't even got a strategy! What would our leader say?

SHE FOLDS AND UNFOLDS HER ARMS RAPIDLY.

No phone. Right. This is not a time to panic. The trouble is my thoughts never seem to come in the right order when I want them to, and look at me now!

FADE IN SOUND OF BUS.

Oh listen! Oh no! I'm too late! It's not a car. I know that sound. It's a bus. The bus! My daughter comes home from school at quarter to five. Disaster! I knew I shouldn't have waited; hot iron or no hot iron!

I really have to move fast now. The bus stops right outside our house! Any moment, Chloe is going to come bounding through the door, right in the middle of it. That would be it! You see, she wouldn't realise until it was too late. I can hear her outside now.

SHE CLENCHES HER FISTS.

There's nothing to hand that's of any use to me! Just shelves of cookery books and small tins. Aah, now there's a sharp object! Right, I'll use that. It's one of those silver retractable pencils, one of the old-fashioned ones where the lead keeps breaking. Anyway, at least it's very sharp.

Uh-oh, she's at the gate. See?

SOUND OF KEY TURNING IN LOCK.

Now I can hear her key turning in the lock. Here we go!

SHE SITS DOWN AND WRITES ON A PAD.

Sorry, I've got to get on with this or they'll leave me, and it will all have been for nothing.

SHE WRITES FRANTICALLY.

There, that's better. Any minute now, Chloe's going to come crashing in, and I know exactly what she's going to say. It'll be: "Mum, you're not writing another one of your crime stories are you?"

CURTAIN.

7. JULIET'S DILEMMA

Julia hovered by the partly open front door waiting for her school friends to arrive. She could see the bus stop from her house. It wouldn't be long before the 8:42 turned up, and they could walk the last few hundred yards to school together. She couldn't wait to surprise them with her good news. She had it all planned. She would wait till her friends arrived at the bus stop, skip out of the house down to the gate, and then tell them all about her success, and how unexpected it was for someone like her. As that last thought crossed her mind, she took a couple of steps back from the door.

She could hear her mother chattering away on the phone to Auntie Eileen.

'The uniform's lovely. It is expensive but very nice. We're taking Julia shopping this Saturday so she can be fitted out... Well, it was all such a surprise!'

Of course, it wasn't a surprise for Julia, but she couldn't tell them that. Auntie Eileen had visited them the previous week to attend Julia's First Communion and had had a long conversation with Sister Angelique after the ceremony. Sister Angelique was her favourite teacher, but now when she thought of her, she felt pangs in her stomach that she'd never experienced before.

There are winners and losers in every contest; and this was a contest after all. But she must be sensitive because not everyone would be able to rejoice at her success. Those girls who hadn't had the same good news as her would be feeling desperately unhappy, so it wouldn't be fair to boast in front of them. She could boast to Melissa though, and

Melissa would jump for joy. It would be just perfect if Melissa were the only one at the bus stop.

The thrill of victory was hot in her stomach as she opened the door a little wider, hearing the February birdsong and the grumbling of a distant train over her mother's voice. She peered urgently down the road, but none of her school friends were visible; the bus would be along soon.

Unlimited treats were in store for her, including sleepovers with her best friend Melissa, but her biggest thrill at having passed the entrance exam to St Augustine's School for Girls was that she would be going to the same school as her. The prospect of being separated from her best friend had felt unbearable, so Julia considered she had every reason, if not right, to feel elated. When the news was announced to all her family and friends, everyone agreed that she had passed against all odds and expectation. That wasn't being unkind or unfair. She had never found reading and writing easy and had been described as a "plodder", so whenever she achieved something, however small, it was always rewarded and celebrated. Sister Angeliqué said she had a sunny disposition. It was a term she became familiar with long before she even knew what a "disposition" was.

Although the entrance exam was intended for the privately educated girls in the city, revision pointers were published so that pupils from any school could try for a place. However, various committees had raised questions as to whether Shakespeare should be such a major part of the junior school curriculum, and if so, whether it should be presented in such detail. But the ambitious parents of the brightest girls always won the debate: the sort of parents who generally serve on committees. All the girls in Julia's year sat the St Augustine exam as a matter of course. This was also discussed by the committees, and the same interested parties argued that the experience gave the pupils a more universal insight into the wide spectrum of academia.

The entrance exam was held at a small number of locations, including the junior school attended by Julia and Melissa. Many of the children taking the exam came from other local schools, and Julia was impressed by the number of children competing for so few places. Many of the pupils from her school spent the majority of the hour-long exam staring into space, not having understood much beyond the rubric. Only a handful of very bright students, like Melissa and Megan, stood any chance of getting through. Or so everybody thought.

At last she could see some of her fellow pupils coming down the road. She pushed the door wider and spotted Megan and Trish in the distance. She watched them come nearer and noticed they were walking quite slowly.

'Perhaps Megan is consoling Trish,' she thought. 'That's kind of her.'

Funny that Trish would be so upset though: she wasn't one of the bright girls, so hadn't expected to do very well. On the other hand, it was assumed that Megan would pass the entrance exam with flying colours. But as they drew nearer, she could see to her surprise that Megan was crying and Trish was consoling her. It hadn't occurred to her that Megan could have missed out on a place in that most prestigious of schools. She thought of all the times that Megan had been rewarded with gold stars for homework, when she herself had struggled and been given half marks or less. Megan's family lived in a big house, and so she was always very generous. She had even invited Julia and Melissa to her birthday party, which was very pleasant with presents for everyone at the end.

Julia dropped her head for a moment and thought about her First Communion and Sister Angeliqué. She gently closed the door.

There had been two parts to the exam: English and maths. The sisters laid on a voluntary after-school maths class for anyone who wanted to brush up their skills. Sister Angeliqué had at first tried to dissuade Julia from attending and warned her not to get her hopes up, but still she persisted. The class was held on Tuesdays and Thursdays, and Julia gave up her horse-riding lessons so she could attend both sessions. Her parents re-iterated the same point made by Sister Angeliqué, which led to the suspicion in Julia's mind that some communication on the matter had come from the school. But going to both classes worked for her as she found the Thursday sessions reinforced her understanding of the material covered on Tuesday's. She also discovered that if she did Tuesday's homework straight after class, she stood a better chance of remembering it. Although her efforts didn't send her straight to the top of the class in school, she could now understand the reasons behind her mistakes when she made them. The improvement was noticeable to her teachers.

She liked the extra classes: they were quiet and still, unlike normal lessons. The sisters were very good at making their subjects fun and lively, but Julia found she worked better in a calm atmosphere and liked doing her homework in an empty classroom. However, the auxiliary staff weren't as happy and turned her out of the room the first time she tried it. Since then, she had become more careful, listening at classroom doors for any cleaning activity that might be going on. Then she would go to the furthest classroom, switch on the light, and settle down to work. Occasionally, she had to dive into a cupboard when she heard someone coming or secrete herself behind a wide teacher's desk. She would hear a grumble or a "tut-tut", and the light would be switched off, only for her to switch it on again when the coast was clear.

Although she had missed going horse-riding, she found an excitement in tiptoeing around the school after everyone had gone home. During her explorations, she would take a look in broom cupboards or peer round the back of the audio-visual equipment that none of the girls were allowed to touch when it was being used in class. There were interesting shelves in the science room, a recess full of dry ingredients in the cooking area, and a number of cupboards and pigeon-holes outside the staff room. These too opened up and spread their secrets wide to her prying eyes.

She knew she was doing something wrong. Sister Angeliqué had a word for the sort of people who did what she was doing and said that no good ever came of it. Before her recent confirmation, Julia had gone to her First Confession. She had thought of something she really wanted to say, but when she imagined kind Father Jim and what he might think of her, she shuddered. She also wondered if he would tell the sisters, even though during confirmation classes he had promised he would never do anything of the sort. If she had confessed properly, and he had done so, she would have wanted to die. She breathed deeply as she knelt down and deciding to keep her sunny disposition, she said something about making faces at Sister Frances during Wednesday's Mass. She was glad she didn't yet go to confession on a regular basis. Perhaps one day, years hence, she would go and confess to someone. Anyway, as God loved her unconditionally, there was no need to confess any big things. She was doing so well with her lessons, and God must have noticed that. Anyway, the feeling of not wanting to hurt Megan sort of made her a good person, didn't it? So that was all right then.

Melissa had helped her to prepare for the exam because she was just as worried about their impending separation as Julia. Melissa seemed to know everything about Shakespeare, and the Shakespeare essay was the hardest part. She had also coached her in maths. Melissa was brilliant at maths, even better than Sister Theresa. She was brilliant at everything. That was why Julia loved her so much.

She dared to open the door a crack, and two more girls came into sight. It was Lizzie and Lizzie. The two girls with the same name who decided it would be such fun to be best friends as well; and it was. They weren't as much friends as Julia and Melissa though, everybody knew that. Sometimes Sister Angeliqué would give a stern look and ask if anyone had a crowbar she could use to prise them apart, which made everybody laugh. The two Lizzies didn't seem like they were having much fun as they walked past. It looked as though they had failed as well. She eased the door open ever so slightly and listened.

'Oh well, St Augustine's not the be all and end all,' said Lizzie.

'Exactly,' replied Lizzie, 'and at least we'll still be together, and the other schools are just as good.'

'Gosh,' she thought, 'I'm going to have to wait and see who's on the next bus.'

It was true: there were a lot of very good fee-paying schools in the area. But St Augustine's was special. If you went there, everybody knew you had to be clever because the exam was so difficult to pass. Julia closed the door again, not wishing to intrude on their disappointment.

'Gosh,' she thought, 'I'm going to have to wait and see who's on the next bus.'

There were no after-school English classes. If there had been, Julia would have gone. Over the course of the three months leading up to the exam, she had worked on her spelling. That was the one thing that had been holding her back. Every time a misspelled word was highlighted, she would write it out ten times and test herself daily from a list of them. Essays were a problem. If she could prepare for something and make notes, she could put her thoughts in order, but every time they had an unprepared essay exercise in class, she did very badly. So she would go home, redo it, and then it would be good, but she could never get it together without the opportunity to really prepare.

The Shakespeare play wasn't overly hard to understand. They were told they had it easy this year with *Romeo and Juliet*. As long as she didn't have to read it out loud in class, she got on well with it in her English lessons.

'It's not as bad as *Antony and Cleopatra*,' warned Sister Frances, 'but that means they'll expect you to go into it in greater depth.' Julia's heart sank. There had to be another way.

A bus pulled up, and she pushed the door wide open as three girls disembarked, and adjusted their bags, ready to walk the last stretch of the school journey. Perhaps one was Melissa. Her heart leapt slightly. She waited till they came closer and squinted at them.

No, it was Jade, Becky and Rachel. Well, Rachel would have definitely got in: she was almost up there with Melissa. But there was no spring in her step. She quickly pushed the door shut again and listened.

To her surprise, she heard Jade say, 'It's not so bad, Rachel. You know, you'll always do well wherever you go.'

Julia was astonished. To imagine Rachel could fail was beyond her. This was incredible. Brainbox Rachel hadn't passed the entrance exam to St Augustine's!

'I know, I know,' she heard Rachel reply. 'I'm more amazed about Melissa. You'd have expected her to pass if anyone was going to.'

Something didn't make sense.

Julia gripped the door to support herself as Becky chimed in. 'I almost fell down when I heard. Still, at least Melissa and Julia will be together after all.'

Hot tears suddenly blinded Julia.

'True,' said Jade. 'I think it was that rotten Shakespeare essay question on decision-making. It was so bizarre, I couldn't even understand the title. No one could have been prepared for an essay question like that!'

As she fell to the mat sobbing out her grief, Julia remembered that she had thought precisely the same thing about the Shakespeare essay question when she first laid eyes on the paper in the staff resources room the night before the exam.

8. HANS AND THE HACKERS

A good firewall is essential for anyone running a business, so there's no point relying on a free one for security. Hans Schmucksome intended to buy a good hardware version, but instead he spent all his money and more on a 3D Super Printer™. It was the fastest, best, and most up-to-date one available - nothing could touch it. As with all technology, the primary aim was to save time and it would enable him to increase his annual productivity and grow his client base, but as a craftsman, Hans realised he would have to compromise on the finish. He already had more orders than he could manage, and although there was greater competition from factory production, he was determined to have no part of that. He was a shoemaker of the old school. A pair of his made-to-measure shoes should last a lifetime or so he contended. The 3D printer would take all the donkey-work out of the process and enable him to work faster. That way his little establishment would turn a profit going forward.

He breathed a sigh of relief. It had taken him ages, but finally the measurements for the shoes were complete. The wives of two landed dignitaries were due to collect the finished items the following morning. He looked at his computer screen. Morning was just a few hours away and he had yet to overlay the stitching pattern. The intricate parts would still have to be done by hand. There would be no sleeping tonight, he told himself. The rent was due on the premises, and he couldn't ignore his cash flow problem: this was a make-or-break commission.

Both customers were on the town council, and one was the wife of the deputy mayor. The 3D Super Printer™ had arrived at just the right time. It stood in the centre of his workbench looking like a giant grasshopper. He carefully put the leather strips into the raw materials caddy. Then he went to the far corner of the workshop where he had set up his computer on its own little table. He sat in front of it in what he considered to be a very executive swivel chair. The skill, his skill, was to adjust the product image according to the guidelines on the screen. It was a long slow process. He rested his head on his elbows and let out a long breath. He thought about making a cup of tea and closed his eyes for a moment. The computer would take over when everything was lined up. Then all he had to do was oversee the processing by his new printer. He clicked "Start" and let his eyes drift down the screen as the computer scanned the data. When it was complete, he would click the button to start the actual printing task. The firewall he had downloaded from the internet had a small red exclamation mark over it. He wondered if he had noticed it before and yawned. Perhaps he had, perhaps he hadn't, no matter. His breath began to rasp slightly as he leant sideways onto the soft arm of the chair, and he swivelled comfortably.

Church bells rang and echoed around the sharp corners of the cobbled street. Hans woke with a start and counted them as they continued beyond three, four, five, six. He slapped his forehead, swung the chair round, and stared at the computer. Seven, eight! The computer was in sleep mode, as he had been! He had fallen asleep! He thumped the mouse, the screen trundled back to life and displayed a text box: "Task Complete". He looked at it, confused. He couldn't remember starting it, so maybe he had accidently touched something and wasted all his carefully cut leather? This was terrible.

He dashed over to the print bed of the printer. There was nothing there. He stared down at the smooth glass surface. How could it be empty? The exit cavity overhung the other side of the workbench. Its loose cover rose automatically to let the end products tumble out. He had taken out a loan to purchase it, and he dreaded looking inside. If it were blocked up with torn strips of leather, it would probably be beyond repair, and that would be it. They would be out on the streets.

The doorbell rang.

'Oh no!' he mouthed to himself.

He peered inside the cavity, but it was clear. There was no evidence of the leather there or on the print bed. Where could it have gone? The doorbell rang again, and he covered his ears.

'Hans! Hans! The door!' called his wife Gertrude. 'It's Mrs Gruber!'

He stood there a moment, wondering what to say to her. As he turned to answer the door, he tripped. There on the floor, directly under the exit cavity, was a perfect pair of court shoes. He picked up each one and examined it. But... how?

The letterbox banged.

'Hans! Answer the door!'

He examined the stitching: it was his own pattern, but it had been applied all the way round the instep, something he would never have normally taken the trouble to do himself.

'Hans!'

He snapped out of his reverie and went to the front door, where the bell and the letterbox resounded with a regular rhythm.

'I thought you weren't in,' grumbled Mrs Gruber.

She took the shoes from his hand. 'Don't I get a box for them?'

'Oh, umm... well...'

'Hans!' cried his wife. 'Where are your manners? What is wrong with you today? Fetch Mrs Gruber a box! Now!'

Mrs Gruber examined the shoes while he fumbled around on the top shelf of his workshop. All the boxes were flat-packed, except one.

'Simpleton Hans,' said Gertrude. 'That one's too small. I hope you didn't make the same mistake with the shoes! Mrs Gruber, would you like a cup of tea?'

Hans pressed out the sides of a full-sized shoebox, pausing every few seconds to fiddle with the computer. He went back through the programme. All the measurements had been fed in and adjusted exactly to match the variations in the leather, which was most mysterious. He couldn't understand it. He had no memory of doing it himself, and surely he couldn't have carried out such a complicated task in his sleep?

Mrs Gruber smiled broadly over her tea as they admired the shoes.

'Will they do?' he asked.

'Will they do?' she asked in reply. 'Why, they're perfect! So beautiful and so comfortable.' She put them back on. 'I have never owned such a superb pair of shoes. Will they do? Absolutely! I'd like to order two more pairs for next week, please.'

'Will they do?' hissed his wife, after she had gone. 'Simpleton Hans! Will they do?'

'But this is very strange,' he said. 'You see, I didn't make them. I mean I set out all Mrs Gruber's measurements, but I didn't craft them. The computer did that. But how? It's made all the adjustments itself, but I'm sure computers can't do that.'

'Simpleton Hans!' she mocked. 'I don't think you understand computers at all.'

Later that day, he received an order from the mayoress herself. She wanted three pairs of shoes and was very particular about having the same stitching as Mrs Gruber. This was the commission he had been waiting for. It would set his reputation in stone. She invited him to the Civic Hall to measure her feet.

'We have two ambassadors coming next week,' she said. 'I want all my shoes ready for then. Mrs Gruber will be there too. I hope my shoes will be just as fine as hers.'

He scratched his head and wondered how he would find the time. Although it was possible to do it by hand, it would be slow-going. If only he knew what had happened that night when he had fallen asleep in his workshop.

By the time evening came, he had prepared the leather and cut it into rough pieces. He switched on the computer and the 3D Super Printer™. He input the measurements for the cutting stage, reading them from his notes. Then, he placed the first piece of leather in the raw materials caddy to be cut, bit by bit, by raising or lowering the tension according to variations in the material. He clicked his mouse. Nothing happened.

'Oh no!' he thought.

A text box appeared: "INSERT ALL THE LEATHER PIECES". He blinked. The screen changed and another text box appeared: "DO SO NOW".

This was not what the instruction manual recommended because if one piece were placed even a millimetre awry, all the other pieces would be ruined, not to say caught up in the mechanism of the printer itself. He couldn't afford to waste his leather. The screen changed again, and the word "NOW!" flashed insistently at him. Mesmerised, Hans obeyed. He stacked them as carefully as he could until there was no more room. "CLOSE THE LID" read the screen. It wouldn't close properly. The screen changed: "PUSH THE LAST PIECE DOWN AND CLOSE IT". He did as instructed. This was ridiculous! There was no way he was going to start the programme with his fragile printer stuffed to the gills like that. He must show his wife.

'Gertrude!' he called. She was upstairs. He went to the bannister and called her. As she came down, he told her about the strange messages and what he had done.

'You see this? The printing programme seems to be overriding the instruction manual!'

'Simpleton Hans!' she said. 'You'll end up breaking it! Take out all the leather and call the helpline.'

'Oh no! Oh no!' cried Hans as he heard a whirring and grinding sound. 'It's started of its own accord!'

'Can't you stop it?'

'I could stop the computer, but you can't touch the printer until everything's gone through or the bits get stuck!'

'But you said this was the fastest, best, and most up-to-date one available, and that nothing could touch it!'

For an agonising three hours, they watched the printer crunch and grumble. Sometimes it rattled so much, it almost bounced off the workbench, and they held each other tight in fear. Soon, little wisps of smoke began to rise from the mechanism. The shoemaker and his wife hugged each other hopelessly. Then there was silence. The text on the screen read: "PROGRAMME COMPLETE" in large green letters. Then it changed again: "DISPENSING ITEMS".

They looked at each other. As the computer screen faded to black, the printer made a soft whirring sound. The exit cavity opened, and, one by one, ten shoes flopped out onto the floor. Five perfect pairs. Without a word, they laid them out on the workbench. When he buffed them with a cloth, the leather almost glowed. It was nigh on impossible to see the stitching, but when Hans looked through a magnifying glass, he almost cried when he saw his own patterns so perfectly aligned in miniature.

'It seems to have a mind of its own!' he said.

'What a pity you don't,' she replied.

The recipients were all delighted but none more so than the mayoress. Later that week, Hans was asked to supply footwear to all the visiting ambassadors and their wives. They were so pleased with the shoes that, to the joy of all the traders in the town, a trade deal was signed with the neighbouring countries. More and more orders came in. Hans had to install a second printer and still the same thing kept happening: the programme did all the skilled work better than he ever could. Months went by and they became rich. One day his wife made a discovery.

'You know, Hans,' she said, 'it isn't actually the programme guiding the work. It's something online. A third party of some sort.'

'What do you mean? Another programme? An app or an upgrade or something?'

'No,' she said mysteriously. 'Look at your firewall. That exclamation mark means it's been breached. You've got a virus. We can trace it with Googlewire. Here, look, I'll set it up, and you run the programme for a pair of shoes.'

Googlewire was a tracking device that could locate the source of any malicious activity and provide a map reference. While the shoes were being made, it sent them an email with a grid reference for a location in Kurdistan.

'Well, that's interesting,' said Hans, 'but not much use. We can't go off to Kurdistan and see for ourselves.'

'Simpleton Hans!' she replied. 'We'll use the satellite view on Google Maps and home in on them there. It will take seconds. Watch.'

Sure enough, they were soon able to see a dilapidated building at the end of a street.

'So this is where my computer virus originated,' said Hans. A few minutes research on Wikipedia told them a little about the village and the poverty of the people who lived there.

'Perhaps that building is a factory. I wonder why they chose to commandeer your computer?'

'I don't know,' replied Hans. 'All I know is that whoever is doing this has been very kind to us. We should do something for them,' he said. 'We should send them money.'

'Simpleton Hans!' chided his wife. 'First, it would probably be stolen on the way. Second, there's political hostility between our two nations. And third, that part of Kurdistan still operates a system of bartering.'

'So what can we do?'

'We'll have to find another way.'

They continued to play with the satellite view, zooming in as close as they could to the factory. They were able to see the back of the building and a park opposite where five men were sitting on a bench.

'That must be them!' said Hans. 'The one on the end is holding an awl, and see the one in the middle? That's a good old pair of lasting pincers in his lap. We've found them!

'But look how cold they must be. There's snow on the ground, and they've all got holes in their coats.'

'Then I'll tell you what we'll do, we'll make them some warm coats.'

'How will we know what size to make them?'

'If you look closely, you can see that the awl and the lasting pincers look quite big in their hands. But I know that those tools are the same size as my own, so I can tell they must be small in stature. I'm sure they'll be grateful for good sturdy clothing. We'll make it by hand.'

The couple set to work on the coats and made several in different styles and colours. They stayed up late working into the night, but they didn't mind as the hackers were saving them so much time meeting their orders. When they had finished, they laid them out on the workbench and admired them.

'These will keep them warm in the coldest winters,' said Hans.

'They'll be so pleased with us,' said his wife.

'How will we know they've got them?'

'Simpleton Hans! I'm going to book an international courier that will guarantee to get them there in only five days.'

'So he'll come back and tell us what they say, will he?'

'Simpleton Hans! The building opposite has a webcam, so we can watch the delivery live!

Five days later, the pair received a text message from the courier to say the delivery was about to take place. They switched on the computer and clicked on the webcam site. They had a clear view of the empty street. The couple watched the courier put the box of coats down and ring the bell. Then he got in his van and drove away.

For a moment, nothing happened, and the shoemaker and his wife began to worry. Perhaps the workers had gone or perhaps they had the wrong address. A cat slunk across the road and stared at the camera. As they watched it, the door opened and the box was pulled inside.

'Look, the box is gone!' Hans said. 'We missed it!'

'Simpleton Hans, distracted as always by the inconsequential. Wait!'

Suddenly, the door burst open, and five short men came out wearing the new coats. They stood cheering and admiring each other in the middle of the road. Then they slapped each other on the back and put beer bottles to their lips. Hans and Gertrude watched as the men danced out of sight. The shoemaker and his wife continued to stare at the empty road until darkness fell and the webcam switched itself off. They went into the scullery to make a cup of tea, feeling very satisfied with their good deed.

The Kurdistan cobblers never hacked into his system again. Hans had to do his own programming and stitching by hand as he had always intended. Fortunately, he had learnt from their example and was able to do his own tiny patterns all the way round the instep.

After a few months, he regretfully signed up for an annual subscription to a commercial firewall. He would never be hacked into again because it was the fastest, best, and most up-to-date one available - nothing could touch it.

9. PONDOODLE'S GONK

"He was a disappointed man." That's what it should have said. I don't remember what it actually says, but it certainly doesn't say that. You can go and see for yourself, if you like. You'll find it next to the church in a little village just outside Keighley, if you can be bothered. What was he disappointed in? Life? Love? Career?

'So you think you want to marry my daughter, do you then?'

'Aye sir. I know I want to, and Ginny is as keen as I. With your permission of course, Mr Canon.'

The older man rubbed his long chin as he spoke. 'You're not a wealthy man, Mr Pondoodle.'

'I have prospects, sir.'

'Prospects, Mr Pondoodle, can't be eaten any more than they can be held up to the light and shown. We are Dissenters, and as you know, Mr Pondoodle, it is hard work and hard work alone that impresses us.'

Although Mr Roland Canon was a small man with a bald pate and a little snub nose, he held some authority in his gait. When he looked up at a fellow, as he invariably did, he exuded an expectation of improvement in that fellow's attitude and respect.

On the other hand, Derek Pondoodle always felt that he was in the wrong even when exchanging no more than a morning or evening greeting with his neighbour.

'When I get my next patent, sir, I will be working very hard advertising and organising the manufacture of my product.'

'Hmm, buttons.'

'Aye, sir, but buttons such as no one has ever seen.'

Derek Pondoodle hadn't had much schooling, but in this age of new machines and new systems, he learned voraciously, driven by dreams of being a great inventor. As soon as he had the freedom to do so, he set himself up with a workshop in his father's garden and began to forge ahead. His first patent was for a top hat with square ventilators in the sides to let the air flow in and out. When he sold this to a manufacturer, he was able to afford the various tools and mechanical devices that allowed him to experiment with different woods and metals. He invented a cart that went before the horse, which had three tilting wheels fixed to a rotating plate so that the two wheels touching the ground would be the ones turning and, in doing so, would always turn in the direction the horse was proposing to move. When the patent for this was finally granted, he made something of a show of himself by taking his contraption about town. Thus, he became known to a great many people in various spheres of influence; though he was not always considered as serious a contender as he would have liked. His symmetrical buttons that needed no buttonholes had reached the demonstration stage well before any interest had been shown in the fore-cart.

That there was a surfeit of demonstration and a deficit of application was of concern to Mr Canon when he considered the future happiness of his daughter, but he realised she could have fixed her heart on far worse than Derek Pondoodle. The young man didn't drink, having taken the pledge before he was old enough to start, and he was honest and gentle, but his trade was both precarious and elusive.

This was the age of hard work. The French wars were over and the industrial north was grinding out new products that were sent all over the country and, indeed, the Empire. This was the age of invention, and Derek Pondoodle was an inventor.

His workshop, a low slope-roofed shed built onto the back of his father's cottage, was lit and heated by oil both in winter and throughout most of summer. During the day, it was where he worked and ate. At night, it was where he slept, having fashioned a plank bed that lay flush to the wall lengthways. A neat rack was fixed to its base wherein lay *Tales Of The Arabian Nights* or *The Greek Heroes* or whichever of the books preserved from his childhood he had most recently chosen to read. From these, he took his inspiration. His tools, benches, and pulleys (some cadged or borrowed from factories and outhouses) lined the other wooden walls or hung from the slanting roof. His latest invention tumbled over the workbench as untidily and as wildly as his enthusiasm for it.

The manufacture of clothing was fast becoming mechanised, and the awkwardness of buttonholes added expense and time to production. But Derek Pondoodle had the answer: interlocking discs. Each button had a zigzag edge that looked like a piece of jigsaw puzzle, which could be clipped into its opposite twin with nothing more than a general fiddle and a hard squeeze. The edges themselves, he suggested in his patent application, could be of any shape so long as they fitted together and held the garment in place. His first prototypes, gold and red in colour, were too large to be fashionable because he had made them using a medal stamper, the business end of which he had doctored with a chisel to produce the necessary edge. Since it had been a process of trial and error, as most great enterprises are, the hammer had been worn to half its size. Because of this, the buttons laid out on the shelf extended in shape from nearly round to crescent moon, but only the latter could be successfully clipped together. He had yet to fix them to clothing, but he saw no reason why the northern textile trade should not be revolutionised overnight.

'How did Roland take to your suit?' asked his father, who had been standing at the door.

'With no great enthusiasm,' he replied.

'That can be accounted for,' said his father. 'We went to the new Lord Mayor's parade today, and as he didn't get near the front he couldn't see the carriage, nor did he see the mayor. Great throngs lining the streets as if it were royalty passing through. Roland was forced to stand at the back and I with him. He was in a dark mood after that.'

'Most unfortunate,' said Derek. 'To think, if there had been no parade, I might have been announcing my engagement to Ginny.'

'However things turn out in that regard, son, it may be of some interest to you that there is to be a great exhibition in London. An exhibition of inventions of all varieties and sizes.'

'What is London to me? It will simply be an exercise in which the wealthy sell their own items and promote their own interests.'

'Seemingly not. A royal commission has demanded that we set up a committee right here in Keighley to consider what has been done to better the world. They want articles and ideas from the provinces to put on show for all to see. I would say seize the moment.'

Derek had a fine mattress. It was stuffed fat with horsehair and supplied a soft surface for his plank bed when it was pulled out under the sash window. He had designed it so that as it was pulled out, a geared pulley raised a wooden slat against the glass to prevent the bright moon from keeping him awake. That night, it was his thoughts that did that. How might a man as small as Mr Canon be afforded a fair chance to view a spectacle of interest amidst the taller specimens of his own kind? Possibilities drifted through his night-drowsed mind. He saw a box on wheels being pulled by a rein and pushed by means of a semi-circular grip. There followed a single-seater steam train on which the seat might rise up, first by persuasion of a combustion engine, then by the efforts of the traveller using a system of gears. Stilts with rocking horse feet came next, which were quickly superseded by a harness attached to a crane. Though each of these might have supported and raised the person of Mr Canon, they would not do the same for his dignity. Perhaps he did not wish to levitate above the crowd but simply to pass through it more easily. "Ay, there's the rub," as the great man said. The real question was how to transport small personages through dense crowds whose members lacked the gentility to move aside of their own accord.

Derek Pondoodle woke up as the late August sun began to flood the horizon and the edge of the wooden slat. He spun himself out of bed and rubbed his hands together. As had happened to him on numerous occasions, an idea had formulated in his dreams. A beach sloped down from blue-green cliffs (this particular shade had probably come from a picture book he had been reading), and he dreamed he was walking towards the sea, when a boat suddenly hove into view. Men, women, and children poured off the craft with some urgency and made towards the cliffs while he persevered in walking towards the sea. He would surely have been overwhelmed by the oncoming passengers had he not been saved by a stick he found in his hand. This wonderful article jerked from side to side of its own volition, and the people scattered around him. He sat up in bed, still half in his dream, with both hands gripping the imaginary stick.

It would be a stick that moved in such a way as to batter anything or anyone in its path. Obviously, it would have to be designed so as to not cause injury, but there should still be enough play in its mechanism to allow the bearer to guide the direction of other folk. This, he believed, could be achieved by a rotary method, not unlike that in a bird scarer. A circular handle could be twisted by the owner, which would cause the end of the stick to rock from side to side. It should be sufficiently heavy so as not to cause the upper end to move too much in the grasp and not so heavy as to be impossible to carry. He pushed the silver buttons to one side and laid sheets of blank paper on the workbench. Pi would describe the circumferences of the handle and the arc of the stick, and calculus would reveal the secrets of the action. He scrawled, measured, and ruled lines until the sheets were covered. Then, he hauled up his bed and pinned them over the frame that held his valuable books. The whole morning was then given over to hammers and saws.

Early in the afternoon, his father appeared at the door. As often happened when he started a new project, Derek had not asked for his dinner.

'I've thought about that exhibition, father,' said Derek as he sawed a narrow strip of wood. 'Do you know when the committee is meeting next?'

'Every Wednesday in the town hall a'bleve. Is that there object your new invention?'

'It is, and I will be taking it straight down to them on the very morrow, I can tell you.'

'I think you have to have more than just the item itself,' cautioned his father. 'I think you need sponsorship or at least some evidence of it.'

'Then I know just where to get it. Is Roland Canon likely to be at home this evening?'

'I've no doubt he is, but I don't know as to whether he'd be so kindly disposed to your new invention as to offer financial backing, Derek.'

'We'll see, won't we?'

By the end of the afternoon, he had two prototypes of what he was going to call his "Batty Stick" ready and working. He made his way to the big house at the top of Hangman's Hill where his sweetheart had been born and raised.

'Mr Canon,' he began when the interview commenced, 'forgive me for being so bold, but I have heard of your

104

troubles at the Lord Mayor's parade, and I have come up with a solution.'

'What troubles?' asked the man irritably, having been interrupted at his supper.

'Not being able to see over all the other people,' he replied quickly, still being out of breath from hurrying up the hill.

'I don't know so much about that. I left early because of all the kerfuffle. Extravaganzas and such like have never much held my interest anyway.'

While he was speaking, Derek was putting his device together (it could be converted into a portable state for convenience). He turned the handle sharply, and the machine did as it was meant to so earnestly that the older man had to leap out of the way.

'What do you think you're playing at?' he snapped.

'Sir, if you were part of a close crowd of people, then you and others around you would surely move out of its arc as nimbly as you have just so done.'

'I have no doubt as to the veracity of that, but you don't propose that such a thing is fit to be carried about by folk?'

'Only by persons of a modest height, sir, in order that they may engage in those activities currently enjoyed by persons of a less modest height.' Derek had, from a young age, been brought up to practise the virtue of courtesy.

'What happens when everybody owns one? Do they then have to be designed to be bigger and more threatening? No, Derek. Your buttons were one thing, but this is quite another. If this is meant to impress me as far as regards your suit to my daughter, then I am afraid you are badly mistaken.'

'No, sir,' said Derek, perhaps more firmly than graciously. 'I am looking for sponsorship or at least the prospect of it so that I can go to the committee for the London exhibition with a concrete proposition behind me. I wasn't thinking of Ginny.'

Mr Canon rubbed his bearded chin. This was the first time Derek had, in discussion, demonstrated anything less than a full-hearted concern for his daughter. She was, as they say, the "apple of his eye" and had been so for long enough to see her many contemporaries married and settled over more years than he liked to count.

'I see,' he said. 'You intend to become a part of this "Great Shalimar". I respect your ambition at least. But unless you're from London, they won't take a thing that size; they won't give you the space. No, you will have to make a model, a scaled-down prototype. I'll offer to sponsor you, but I won't be buying one for myself, if it's all the same.'

Though it had taken Derek less than a day to make the full-sized model, the smaller version presented new and more complex problems, so although he worked through the night, he did not have the replica finished until just before the meeting. Armed with Mr Canon's promise of sponsorship and his device, he had to rush to the town hall in order to arrive at the start and therefore gain the best advantage. However, it was not until the end of two very long hours' worth of talking when the chairman asked if there were any other business that Derek could burst forward and present his Batty Stick.

Though tiny compared to the original, it caused no small amount of amusement when it was set up on the table and allowed to knock pencils and rubbers here, there, and everywhere. It cannot be said that many in that room were entirely clear as to the purpose of the clockwork model, particularly when most of the demonstration time had been spent bending down retrieving pencils. But as there was a dearth of contributions from the locality, the committee were inclined to support one of their own at the exhibition. A small red leather-bound book that had been signed by Prince Albert was presented to him in order that he might sign his own name, which he did with a red glow passing over his face.

'What you'll have to do, lad,' said the secretary, 'is provide a little dummy or figurine so that folk at the exhibition can see straightaway how it works.'

'Aye,' said another, 'because they'll be passing by so quick, as folks are wont to do at these things.'

For the rest of the week, there was no man in Yorkshire happier than Derek Pondoodle, and not least because his beloved Ginny had agreed to go to the local fair with him on Saturday. Her father had permitted this partly because of Derek's improved prospects and partly by his abstention from amorous intimations at their recent encounter. Paradoxically, this perceived cooling of interest made Mr Canon less averse to the young man's suit; we humans are paragons of the paradox. That being the case, Derek Pondoodle found himself greeted warmly when he arrived at the house on Hangman's Hill. He felt quite warm himself when he saw Ginny, who was dressed in a green muslin dress with a matching silk hat bordered with red flowers that matched her ruby lips. Mr Cannon had even commissioned the pony and trap to take the pair to the fair that fine afternoon.

It must be stated that the vagabonds of Loughton have long been famed as the meanest pack of thieves in Essex. The menfolk traded in horses, and the women, when they were not stealing from the villagers, fashioned toys and dolls from whatever they could find, selling them to whoever would either be willing to buy or fearful of not doing so. In those superstitious days, the curse of Saint Patrick would cause the stomachs of even the boldest of Essex men to tremble, so much so that every country cottage had a cabinet or a mantelpiece adorned with at least one of these useless trinkets of kerbside manufacture. Such enterprises led some of these vagabonds to travel well beyond the boundaries of the county, and they were often to be found at the local fairs.

It was at a coconut shy, while encouraging his sweetheart to divest herself of a small missile in the direction of a fine example of that fruit, that Derek Pondoodle became fascinated by the prizes. A row of goblinesque figures stared down at him from a shelf above the targets: quirky little faces affixed to short bodies, long gangly arms, and legs invisible below the stoop of their midriffs. These fair creatures (nothing more than a collection of discarded bottles and rags) were known as "gonks", taken from an obscure Middle Eastern word for "monkey". These Loughton ladies ensured that the cost of the prizes hardly impinged on their profit margins, even in the rare event of a dislodged coconut. As he stared, his darling's first and second attempts fell short of the target. She would have taken up the third and last ball to do the same had his hand not covered it.

'Forgive me,' he said. Picking it up, he hurled it at the hairy target. It struck home, the coconut falling to the grass. She clapped her hands and perused the prizes. Expectations of gallantry on the part of her beloved led her to believe that she might make her choice of the various sweetmeats and novelties displayed, but it was not to be. She watched curiously as he demanded the surliest of contorted visages from the row of gonks.

'This is perfect,' he said to her as they walked towards the Punch and Judy show. 'I can use it to demonstrate my Batty Stick at the London exhibition.'

She took it off him and perused its determined little face. If anything was going to push its way through a crowd, this little imp certainly was.

'You see its arms?' he continued. 'I can fix them round the stick as though it were holding a golf club. There will be a notice to say that anyone who wishes to do so may turn the handle. Anyone close by will hear it and see it in operation. I am rather hoping your father might take the full-size version there himself. I believe he intends to go.'

'Father won't,' she said flatly, remembering the sweetmeats.

*****

The Pondoodle Batty Stick was submitted to the exhibition too late to be included in the *Official Descriptive and Illustrative Catalogue* (as published by the committee), but was promised inclusion in a smaller supplement. This was still not yet available on the day on which Derek, accompanied by Mr Canon and his daughter, arrived in Hyde Park. The older man made a modest investment in the younger by the purchase of tickets at a cost of two guineas each, the train fare to Victoria, and a pony and trap to take them to the venue: there being no train station at Hyde Park.

The strange building stood three storeys high; its arched glass dome glittering in the June sunshine. They walked the concrete forefront alongside a polite crowd until they came to the entrance. The Batty Stick had been placed in the category of "Miscellaneous Manufactures and Small Wares", but due to constraints of space, it had to be exhibited in one of the third storey side galleries. Arriving at the reception desk, Derek enquired about its exact whereabouts and was ushered to one side by an official.

'Mr Pondoodle?'

'Aye,' replied Derek.

'We have a Miss Adelaide Windsor wishing to speak to you.'

Once again, feeling a rise in his prospects at this further indication of progress, Derek soon found himself considering how he might respond to the interest of an established London firm in marketing his invention. Miss

Windsor, it was explained, was the Director of Morals and Christian Integrity for the entire show.

'I wonder,' he reflected, 'what aspect of my invention such a worthy lady might see as advocating morality, as surely she must.'

Mr Canon beamed at his now potentially prospective son-in-law. Only Ginny looked worried.

Miss Windsor differed from the other women present by her perfectly straight, black dress, which was unencumbered by frills or ribbons of any sort.

'Good day!' smiled Derek.

'How dare you!' she seethed. 'How dare you presume to corrupt our proceedings!' She produced his contribution and slammed it on the table. 'You have offended several young women and shamed your own kin with this... this... abomination!'

'But it's a device to enable diminutive persons to get through crowds,' he exclaimed. 'That's all it is, look.' And he twisted the handle.

The little imp began to judder as much as the miniature version had. Due to the design of the gonk, most of the movement took place in its head, emphasising the determined expression of its features even more so than at the fair. Because of the way the creature had been made to appear to grip the end of the stick (rather in the manner one might hold an overly short golf club) at a point just below its stomach, the motion appeared to come from the arms and hands of the creature rather than from gears in the length of the stick. It must also be added that the accompanying notice had been rather too brief in the elucidation of its purpose.

'Ugh!' cried Miss Windsor, throwing her hands across her eyes to protect them from this vulgar display. 'Get him out! Get... him... out!'

Her directions were endorsed by the several assistants who had flanked Miss Windsor during the whole disgraceful proceeding. Despite his protestations, he was none too carefully led from the building. Once outside, it soon became apparent that the gentle Miss Canon and her father had already departed.

We have a custom in these parts, but I don't know if it is still kept up, that if a person inadvertently makes an indelicate allusion, we say, "He has made a Pondoodle's Gonk". The French have a better phrase, I believe. As I say, I can't remember exactly what it says in that little churchyard, but it doesn't tell of his great disappointment. I feel a gravestone should do just that if it is to have anything to do with a man's life.

You may come to Keighley yourself to find out more if you so wish.

10. THE PROSPECTIVE COUNCILLOR FOR BERKDALE EAST

'Come this way.' Mrs Dover walked briskly; her feet seemingly ahead of her elderly body giving Oswald Banfield-Rusk the singular impression that her energy resided mainly in her stout lower half. She was wearing a short checked jacket and constrained trousers of a plain but business-like fawn colour on this slightly overcast August afternoon. This was the afternoon on which Oswald had chosen to keep a promise he had made at a committee meeting some weeks before, otherwise he would never have come to the middle of this estate. She had met him at the entrance to a complex of buildings, architecturally united but built for a variety of designated purposes. They walked down a corridor where the rumblings of soft percussion followed by the dancing lilt of a jolly organ could be heard. She walked firmly ahead ignoring people coming the other way, whether they greeted her or not. Oswald, on the other hand, smiled and nodded as politely as he could.

'Here we are,' she said, pointing. One of a pair of doors opened onto an arena. 'This is what I mean. This is what I have been telling you and the committee for the past year.'

Mr Banfield-Rusk's feet trod softly on the thick carpet. The first thing he noticed was a series of glass cabinets fixed to the nearest wall. He looked closely and saw they contained medals and silver cups. Underneath each one was a little white plaque inscribed with the name of a particular person, a particular year, and a particular dance. The quickstep, waltz, and foxtrot were amply represented. There was also a certificate crediting the establishment with high standards of hygiene and several photos that he presumed were of the most eminent personages of the present organisation. He looked up at the high ceiling from which hung a wide chandelier that flattered the small number of dancers; their deliberate pacing tracing out neat figures to the music he had heard in the corridor. The movements of their feet were nearly soundless despite the wooden floorboards of the dance area, which were so light in colour that they appeared yellow in the brightness of the room. The thick carpet continued around its edges and some way up the skirting of the walls.

'Look at it all,' she said, bringing him out of his reverie. 'No more than a dozen of them.'

To his alarm, Mrs Dover led him onto the dance floor. The gentle music ushering from a Wurlitzer organ caused its operator to lean this way and that as though he too were one of the dancers and not merely the organist. The dancers, mostly women, seemed to be in their mid to late seventies, but they were still able to follow with what could be described as panache the Latin American melodies that rippled exotically from Joe's musical fingers.

'Nice to see you, Beryl!' Joe was more familiar towards Mrs Dover than she would have liked, so she merely nodded in reply.

Although he had been a promising pianist in his schooldays, he discovered jazz during his National Service. When the leisure complex had opened and the locals been taken round in groups, he had been given the opportunity to try the Wurlitzer. The then chair of the council declared they would never find a better exponent of the old ballroom style, and he landed the job by default. It meant that he spent far less time drinking with his old crowd, something for which his wife was truly grateful. She, being one of the regular dancers, waved to Mrs Dover and then whirled round with her partner, another woman.

Mrs Dover introduced her guest to Mr Tyndale, the acting treasurer. Oswald graciously shook his hand and commented on the tasteful decor. Of course, nowadays people did not dance the way they used to. Did Mr Banfield-Rusk dance? Sadly not. Perhaps it was something he might consider in the future? Mr Tyndale took Mrs Dover gently but firmly round the waist and, ignoring the flash of a camera, swam her confidently into the midst of her admiring friends. Oswald folded and unfolded his hands as he stood watching. She deftly turned her partner about then politely released him.

'You see,' she whispered as she returned to his side, 'there are all the lights on and the heating! You won't believe it! Touch the floor... go on.'

Oswald coughed politely and, with a thin-lipped smile directed at no one and everyone, awkwardly bent down to feel the warmth coming through the smooth wood of the dance floor.

'It's heated, you see? In this weather! We never have any more than 12 or 13 in this huge space. It's quite ridiculous! And today's turnout is considered to be a good attendance figure. Then there's Mrs Oakham, the teacher, who comes from out of town, and Joe, who plays the organ for us. They both have to be paid.'

Oswald was expected to answer, but he had been caught off-guard by Mrs Oakham.

'You look like a dancer to me,' she said. 'I hope we'll see you again.'

'Oh, it may happen,' he said, as though not quite comprehending. 'Um, yes... quite.'

'Come on, Oswald,' Mrs Dover stepped lightly to one side and touched his arm. 'There's more to see before we really get our campaign under way.'

'Our campaign?' he asked.

The Banfield-Rusks hailed from Suffolk where their main residence, a rambling manor house that had been in the family for several centuries, stood in the centre of a huge park. Though the family owned, and mostly lived in, various properties in the outskirts of London, Oswald had been brought up there. At 23, and the most recent of the Banfields sired in the family home, he had come down from Oxford not quite sure what he wanted to do. A helpful uncle, who had married late and moved to Berkdale East to be with his young bride, suggested there might be an opening in politics for this fine young man. So not having anything better to do, Oswald decided to throw his hat in the ring, as one does. His uncle organised digs (a three-bedroomed detached new build that virtually threw itself at him) in the same village, and once he felt he could be comfortable there, he began to attend village meetings and events.

Exiting by the same door as they had come in, Oswald and Mrs Dover turned right and followed another corridor around a corner. They had almost passed an adjoining room when, noticing its occupants, she quite brutally swung him 180 degrees and walked him in. This room was smaller with full-length windows that looked out onto flowerbeds and grass that interspersed criss-crossing paths. The clouds had passed over and the sunlight through the windows made the flower arrangers, who numbered four, appear as silhouettes; their efforts filling vases that lined the shelves. They smiled at the visitors as they continued to rustle bunches of dahlias and chrysanthemums that served to make the world a more beautiful place.

'Jolly good,' said Oswald, going slightly up on his toes in homage to their work. He meant it too. He would have liked to have talked to them, but Mrs Dover was in a hurry.

'They all get thrown away,' she said as she ushered him along. 'They're of no use to anyone... Oh hallo, Jean. Jean, this is Mr Banfield-Rusk, our prospective councillor. This is Jean, my neighbour.'

Jean was more slender and possibly younger than his host. Her clothing, a light blue top and green skirt, suggested an unaffected demeanour. Already halfway to laughing, she touched his arm enthusiastically and said, 'I wish you all the best, but I can't promise you my vote.'

'Jean!' said Mrs Dover in admonishment.

'Well...' she replied, spreading her arms by way of apology.

'No, no,' said Oswald. 'An interest in politics is the best one can ask for,' as his uncle had once instructed him to say to wavering voters.

They proceeded in the direction they had previously been going.

'That Jean,' she said, 'thinks she's got a bit of a social conscience or something. Hold it here.'

Mrs Dover had what she called a "bit of a bad leg", so they paused for a moment outside the rooms designated for the "specialist clubs".

'We could always walk a little slower,' he said, trying to show concern for her discomfort.

'I'll be fine in a minute,' she said. 'But look here, I wonder if you might shorten your name for the election. Would you be Mr Banfield? Is that a lot to ask? I think we are more likely get the Jeans of this world on board if you could drop the Rusk for now. So I'm going to introduce you as Mr Banfield.'

Oswald couldn't really see where this was all going, but he certainly wanted to be elected to the council and he certainly couldn't see why he shouldn't. He had always been interested in politics, especially when he listened to Radio 4.

'What about this room?' Oswald felt he ought to ask. The sign said "Specialist Clubs" and the window against which they found themselves appeared mysteriously dark.

'We get youngsters here,' she replied. 'They do things like kung fu on um... Wednesday evenings, I think. At all other times, it's unused; still heated of course.'

'Oh dear,' he said. 'However, the martial arts must be of interest to the young people on the estates around here.'

'Not really. They're all troublemakers and anything they learn in these lessons seems to encourage more fighting at school.'

'Oh dear.'

Turning another corner, they passed the cinema on the left, which was also dark from the outside.

'It's such a shame,' she said. 'They never show the films that people want. Considering they have such an excellent cinema complex in town, one wonders why anyone thought there was a need for one here.'

Oswald couldn't think either and pursed his lips grimly.

On the right and further down was a sub-corridor, which led to a series of little rooms used for therapy and counselling. As they walked down it, an ashen-faced gentleman passed them.

'You know,' said Mrs Dover quietly, 'I've always thought this sort of thing is best left to a proper doctor. People get all sorts of imagined conditions these days. I'm sure I've never heard of half of them. They weren't around when we were young, so where did it all spring from? I don't know, I really don't.'

Neither did Oswald. At least, he didn't think he did.

The gym was in full swing. It was the most popular activity room and was in use throughout most of day. The swimming pool was also popular with mothers (and often their children), though the local schools had their own facilities. It was equipped for hydrotherapy, of which Mrs Dover availed herself whenever her leg played up.

'At the moment, it's very busy because of the school holidays,' she said. 'I do think too many people have been given the free pass. That's something for you to think about.'

Oswald thought about it.

They came out into the warm sunshine. People were walking and chatting among the lawns and flowers; the old and young could be seen mingling; cyclists weaved around mothers hustling pushchairs; and groups of children kicked beach balls, threw Frisbees, or simply ran about. Old men sprawled on benches dozing or smoking in the August air while a plane hummed over the sound of slow traffic. He caught its shadow rushing past as Mrs Dover talked to him about strategy: something about a petition in his name to garner support in the upcoming election. All well and good, he thought.

Over the next few weeks, he attended various council meetings across the area as his uncle had advised. Nothing he saw was as animated as the forthcoming election in Berkdale East, and regular phone messages from Beryl Dover kept him up-to-date with proceedings.

Neighbour Jean wasn't going to sign anything, but then her husband was a strong Labour supporter. However, Mrs Dover, after going up and down the road knocking on doors, triumphantly told her how delighted she was at the support she had been promised.

'Come on, Jean,' she reasoned, 'we all know we need some changes here.'

But her neighbour was strangely unmoved. Several others in the same road did actually deliver on their promise, and the petition went into the local shops and workspaces. Doreen Carter, Mrs Dover's other neighbour, even put a notice in her window inviting passers-by to sign it, and the result went beyond all expectations.

Oswald, who by then had gone back to Suffolk, had a letter from her explaining the next stage of the campaign, so he phoned his uncle for help. His uncle used a Freedom of Information request to find out how much of their council tax was spent on the whole complex. Further investigation found the gym was the biggest drain on resources.

'Right,' said Mrs Dover, when she finally managed to get a meeting with him. 'We have to word this very carefully to make it clear who is responsible for the wastage.'

'Right,' said Oswald.

The petition was presented to the weary councillors, and various promises were made. The ward had been Labour for nearly 40 years. Oswald's uncle had a hotline to the Gazette, and all Oswald had to do was send him the minutes of the council meetings. His uncle worked on the detail and then sent them to the editor. None of the councillors knew of this and the following few months were a nightmare of frustration and failure for them. There was nothing the council could say or do that didn't appear as a bleak headline of impending disaster. That council tax would have to rise was made quite clear, but the reason that this was outside of the council's power was not. Mrs Dover's criticisms of wastage in the running and use of the leisure complex were at the centre of the debate, if a one-sided editorial could be described as such.

Desperate for a positive report, one of the old guard organised a family fun day on the lawns. Acting on his uncle's advice, Oswald turned up during the last half hour and auctioned a compost bin for an environmental cause. The local paper printed a full colour photo of him shaking hands with the winner just above the article, and one could easily have been mistaken in thinking that he had organised the whole event. Oswald's uncle also helped with some of the letters that featured on the middle pages. Even Oswald, getting the hang of it, had a go too. Mrs Dover could usually find a congenial local to put a name to a letter.

When the election happened, there was indeed change. On leaving their positions after so long, many of the old guard moved away. Their remaining supporters felt a combination of hopelessness and incomprehension they had never known before: their enemy having been so utterly intangible to them. Post-mortem discussions failed to determine a cause for their terrific defeat, and their brave new world seemed to have become an unpredictable, indeterminable place overnight. However, Councillor Banfield-Rusk's efforts were duly commended by the new incumbents, and he attended as many meetings as he could, despite having moved a fair distance from Berkdale East. It was only when he was elected leader of the council that he purchased a second property, enabling him to be closer to the locality once more, to the unbounded joy of proud Beryl Dover.

Dance classes ceased. The constant barrage of criticism had affected attendance. The management committee, constantly trying to save money, had to cancel all lessons. The old organist was left with little to talk about with his friends, despite spending more time in the pub with them. The counselling sessions were ridiculed and focus groups disbanded. It was decided that if the clientele needed counselling sessions, they could pay privately for them. No one did. It wasn't possible to find a use for the small rooms, so they were cordoned off to discourage vandalism. The wooden dance floor began to warp when the underfloor heating was turned off that winter. The damage was not identified until the following spring, but the repair costs were found to be prohibitive. The cinema went over to "art" films that attracted strangers, mainly men, from out of town. The gym underwent a big cost-cutting exercise and the pool was closed.

Mrs Dover wanted to talk to Oswald about that, but he was either too busy or away on business. The petitioners had had their day. Oswald was found to have been as good as his word, better even. He made a highly elaborate speech about the mistakes made regarding the leisure centre and the idiocy and lack of financial accountability of its founders. The running and organisation of the enterprise had been put in the hands of people who weren't responsible for paying for it. That, he concluded, was the crux of the matter, and it would have to be reopened with the help of private enterprise.

Over the course of several weeks, the Gazette published his jubilant promises under various headlines espousing common sense. A reopening would mean, of course, a closure: something that hadn't been particularly emphasised in his original speech. The latter took place very quickly, but the former ran into some difficulty as the developers, who had promised to build a new improved complex, went bankrupt after taking the initial payments. It was not immediately possible to ascertain whether any other developer would be willing to take on the project since they would have to underwrite the community benefits promised at the closure of the previous establishment. Compromise was the order of the day, breezed the Gazette, and in the end a new housing estate was planned for the site.

During the course of these events, Oswald was elected onto the city council, which was, conveniently, nearer to his main residence, but politics had begun to bore him. Sometime later, he found himself on the same board of developers that had taken on the site of the old leisure complex. He was taken round it again two years after he had left East Berkdale. He couldn't remember that much about it, but he remembered Mrs Dover.

'Do you know what happened to her?' he asked his guide. No one did.

Mrs Dover, like many, had imagined it would only be a short while before the new leisure centre opened, so she was not unduly sad when it closed.

'They ought to have kept the gym and the pool,' she said to Jean.

When Jean moved to be with her daughter in Salisbury, the young couple who bought the house remained strangers to her. Mrs Dover, not having a family of her own, missed Jean, and though she promised to come back and visit, she never did. Doreen, her other neighbour, became so ill that

Mrs Dover had to do her shopping. When Doreen died, she found herself living with newcomers on either side. They were polite but no more than decency required. The first thing they did was raise the height of the garden fences. When her leg got bad, she found it hard to get all the way to the high street and back for her shopping, so she sold her house and moved to a small flat nearer the town centre. There was a small general store nearby that sold necessities, but there was no community to speak of. Getting out and about became a real struggle, and she noticed that the buses weren't as regular as they used to be. Her friends had dispersed or died, so even if a new leisure centre were to be built, she didn't see what use it would be to her. She occasionally wrote to a relative or phoned a nephew or cousin bemoaning the lack of interest shown towards the elderly of Berkdale East. However, it soon became clear from the awkwardness in their responses that they had limited time for her, and her efforts to keep in touch tailed off scornfully. The second winter after the closure of the complex, the weather was unusually cold. She could only get down to the store with the help of a stick, and when she became ill, it was difficult to find anyone who would shop for her. Her death must have occurred sometime over Christmas, but the exact date would never be known because she was only discovered when the postman noticed a bad smell.

11. IRKWELL'S VIRTUAL SYSTEMS LTD

Doreen Ballchafer's blotchy calves marked the first appearance of her mighty heft to several raincoated persons rushing down the main road of a certain market town. It was noon on a Thursday. As she heaved herself out of the back of the taxi, dirty rain dribbling down the kerb speckled the red skin between the straps of her high-heeled shoes. Her husband bent forward to pay the driver the exact amount, and she began to castigate him.

'Look at your collar. Can't you sort it out? We're there now, come on.'

He grumbled and pushed her proffered hand away. They hobbled along the wet pavement: he mumbling to her and she moaning back at him. He wished she would keep her voice down sometimes.

'This is why you get passed over all the time,' she panted loudly. 'That and because you always have to be so nice. None of these people appreciate it. They're all too stupid. It's about time you realised that, Ernest. Why don't you ever talk to the right people?'

Still bickering, they made their way up the town hall steps to the entrance. She stumbled along next to him, gathering her skirt about her wide girth as modestly as she could in the brutal wind.

'You must be careful what you say to these people,' he said. 'You know, it's really about what you don't say rather than what you do.'

'So what did Mr Bowler-Bullen not say to inveigle himself into the top position when he has half your experience and even less brains?' She waved her podgy hands to shape the absurdity of it.

He walked a little way behind her as she bent forward for balance in a bovine manner on the steep steps that led up to the town hall. They stepped through two swing doors onto a brown-striped carpet where they were met by a regalia-clad and top-hatted doorman, who bowed politely and ushered them into the conference centre. The brown stripes ceased at the entrance and were replaced by a utilitarian beige carpet with faint leaf patterns. The windowless, oblong room had a wood-panelled surround and a table in the middle that stretched to the far end. A sparse buffet was laid out on a smaller table where several staff stood ready to serve from it and the array of glasses half-filled with red or white wine. A young barmaid offered flutes of champagne to Ernest and his wife.

'Aah, Ballchafer!' Graham Brooks, the Finance Director, sported his usual grin. Ernest saw it broaden when he regarded Doreen. 'And your charming wife, I presume?'

Ernest replied curtly but not without the expected decorum, and the pair moved to the buffet table to try to get away from him.

'Hold on to your drink,' continued Graham, following them. 'Did you know we're expecting Basil himself? There's going to be a toast, so I propose grabbing a glass of red as well. You know what this lot are like.' He gave a little jig from above the waist as he said this.

Ernest tut-tutted quietly.

'Not Robinson then?' asked Doreen.

'Apparently not.' Graham had an insistent grin. Ernest avoided his merry eyes.

'Didn't think it was worth leaving Portugal for this then?' she asked. 'Even though it's his company.'

'Now, Doreen,' warned Ernest.

'He's a highly respected sleeping partner,' said Graham, though the emphasis on "highly" suggested that it was others in the firm rather than himself who afforded Robinson that level of respect. Doreen did not understand his sarcasm. He took a glass of red wine from the buffet table and held it in front of one of the young staff, who topped it up from a bottle. He kept it there until it had been filled nearly to the brim. Holding both of his drinks with exaggerated care, he led the couple to the centre table.

'Aah,' said Ernest, 'at last we can sit down.'

Graham hadn't finished. 'The champagne's bloody awful, don't you think?'

'It usually is, but Robinson Irkwell has paid for this out of his own pocket, and I for one appreciate that,' said Doreen, shuffling her mighty posterior into the chair with unexpected difficulty.

'Good for you.' Graham's grin almost exceeded his face, Ernest noted.

Once they were in their seats, the barmaid started refilling the flutes, and Graham moved to a seat at the far end.

'Look at the state of him!' said Doreen. 'He's a complete lush! I think they should get rid of him.'

'Keep it down!' said Ernest. 'They don't need to: he's retiring soon. That's why he can say and do what he likes.'

Bob Cobble from Administration sat next to Ernest and began talking in a loud voice to someone on the other side of the table. Ernest raised his eyebrows.

'I've never liked him,' said Doreen, gesturing towards Cobble. 'His eyes are too close together.'

'Darling!' hissed her husband.

The doorman reappeared. 'Basil Irkwell,' he announced. The fourteen men and eight wives or partners stood as a body. A rake of a man with a bald head and a wild untidy moustache turned towards them from the door.

'Sit down,' he called, gesturing with his hands. His young wife stayed back holding a large square package as he marched towards the executive seat at the top of the table.

He did not fix his gaze on any of them, least of all the unfortunate Tommy Leveridge from Sales, who realised too late that he had sat in that very place and began to vacate it forthwith.

'No. Don't get up again,' said Basil. He moved to the next seat, pleased to have had a chance to demonstrate indulgence. Bowler-Bullen, the new Chief Executive, coughed.

Doreen pushed Ernest's arm. 'Bowler-Bullen is another idiot,' she said as loudly as before. 'He's done nothing at all. You're the one who's made all the money for them. He's just a passenger, and yet he gets to be Chairman of the Board.' Her husband had something of a coughing fit as the son of the founder (and main shareholder) prepared to address them.

'Just a few words before the buffet,' said Basil. Though he was a thin man, his round belly was apparent when viewed from an angle. Doreen noticed a mole on his chin and made a point of remembering it so she could refer to it when she regained Ernest's attention. This was the sort of thing he never noticed. It was no wonder he hadn't been short-listed. She watched the mole closely. As Basil Irkwell talked, it moved about as though applying the necessary apostrophes and full stops on his behalf.

'My father regrets that he couldn't be here today on the twentieth anniversary of our firm. But he has asked me to say how proud he is of our achievements, particularly in the past couple of years since we opened up to the overseas market. To mark the occasion, he has asked me to give you this little token of his gratitude for all your hard work.'

Mrs Irkwell, a tall slender woman with long dark hair, stepped forward without smiling. The closer she came, the clearer it was that she was his junior by many years. She put the package on the table in front of the new Chief Executive.

126

Doreen made a face and nudged Ernest. 'Look at her fat legs,' she said.

'Come on, Bullen!' called Ernest.

'Oh, yes... of course,' said Peregrine Bowler-Bullen arriving belatedly at realisation. He took the package and placed it on the desk. Doreen nudged Ernest again all too obviously, and he tried to edge away from her.

'As our new Chief Executive, I believe it's intended that you open it,' said Graham Brooks, still with his grin.

Graham was in his late fifties and was shortly due to retire as Finance Director. He and Ernest had been Peregrine's rivals for the top position on the Board, though his own application had been rather more half-hearted than that of the other two

'Oh, yes... of course,' repeated Peregrine. He began to delicately peel the tape from the brown paper.

He opened it, miraculously managing to keep the wrapping in one piece.

'Come on, man,' said Basil. 'We haven't got all day.'

He respectfully folded the paper while glancing at Basil Irkwell.

The gift was a seated Robinson Irkwell painted in oils. Ernest was the first to begin clapping.

'It's quite wonderful,' enthused Peregrine. 'It should go on the wall at the bottom of the stairs.'

'Good heavens, no,' said Graham. 'It must have pride of place in your office. Get rid of that old galleon.' Peregrine glowered at him.

The buffet was uncovered and the guests milled politely around it. Ernest had been among the first to get to the food, but when his wife poked him in the back, he obediently retreated. By the time he took his turn, the little sausages on sticks had gone. His wife sat down opposite Tommy Nixon from HR. Tommy had a plate piled high with quiche slices, sausages, chicken wings, and crisps. Like her husband, Doreen had a small portion, which she picked at demurely, something that ladies of the larger persuasion are wont to do. This can lead the rest of us to believe that obesity is a result of breathing in fat from the air. However, that very morning, she had devoured a huge breakfast consisting of all that is traditional to the English in culinary extravagance. Ernest took his plate of cheese puffs and a sandwich to a chair between her and Tommy. Basil made his way over to them with a glass of wine.

'Ah, hallo, hallo,' said Ernest.

Basil nodded at him and gave a small grunt that seemed to indicate satisfaction with what he saw in the man but no more. His attention was on Tommy Cobble.

'We really ought to call one of you "Tom",' he said. 'That would avoid confusion, wouldn't it?'

'Oh yes, sir,' said the man from HR. 'What a very good idea! I shall put it to the others.'

Ernest felt another poke. His wife pointed first at the picture and then at Basil.

'Umm, it's a fine picture,' he said. 'All sorts of… good colours and tones, I notice.'

'Art lover, are you?'

'Er… no. Well, yes and no… Sort of.'

'Perhaps you know the artist?'

'Well, I might…'

'Rodrigo Santiago.'

Ernest touched his chin. 'Rodrigo Santiago… Rodrigo Santiago. I wonder if… maybe…' he nodded slowly. Peregrine sidled up cautiously.

Basil smirked. 'Give it up, chap. He's a local in Dad's village. That's not even his real name. It's Jim something-or-other! He's as English as you or me!'

'Aah!' said Ernest as Peregrine sniggered. Doreen leaned towards them, taking an interest in her husband's conversation with the firm's second largest shareholder.

'What about you, Perry?' went on Basil. 'All those targets to meet now! Any regrets?'

'It's the rise in the price of oil that's going to make things difficult,' replied Peregrine. 'We would have been able to turn it around, but if a barrel of oil stays at $80, it isn't going to be.... well... straightforward, as it were.'

'I'd be surprised if that's the case,' said Doreen, seizing her chance. 'You can easily put up your consultancy fees to cover it. The success you all had last year means demand is going to stay high. I'd be very surprised if you didn't beat all the targets.'

'Good,' said Basil. 'We should have you on the Board.'

'I do like to keep in touch,' she said as Peregrine reddened.

The champagne ran out all too quickly, so Basil and his wife left early. Graham sidled up behind Ernest before he could escape. He handed him a glass of red wine.

'Don't get too squiffy,' he said. 'On the other hand, you might be fun later on!'

'It's my first drink actually,' said Ernest. 'I didn't touch my champagne.'

'I'm surprised anyone did,' said Doreen. 'Where was Robinson anyway? It was his do. He founded Irkwell's. What has Basil ever done?'

'Oh,' Graham breathed out thoughtfully, 'you know, ponced around, spent money, that sort of thing. When you've got more of it than sense, what else can you do? He does always manage to appear important though. Ought to give him a knighthood or something, I say.'

'You won't see Robinson at these sorts of dos,' chimed in Tommy. 'Even though he is technically still a director.'

'He's a sleeping partner,' said Ernest.

'He's well ensconced in Portugal. Why should he ever bother coming back? His new bride is even younger than Basil's missus. I understand he owns part of the Monte Rei golf course. Why miss a game of golf for this nonsense?'

'The fishing's good too, so I've heard,' said Graham. 'He's bound to have his own boat.'

The doorman in the top hat indicated that the taxi that Ernest had requested had arrived.

'Yes, sorry,' he said, regarding the wine in his hand. 'I can't mange this. If anyone wants it, it's going.'

Graham took up his offer with such grace of movement that it might have been part of a dance. Ernest and Doreen made their excuses and followed the doorman.

'Did you see the look on Peregrine's face?' Doreen said to her husband. 'It was like he was chewing a wasp.'

'Maybe, but I wish you'd be more circumspect. Anyway, Basil got me with that picture!'

'He was joking. He likes you, Ernest. You're natural with him. Not like all those other sycophants.'

The windscreen wipers on the taxi whined incessantly all the way home. Once again, the taxi driver got no more than his due.

'What about Mrs Cobble? What did you think of her? I thought she was an utter slattern.'

'I'm going to lie down,' said Ernest. 'That whole charade was lousy, and I've got to work later on.'

His wife settled down in front of the computer. She looked at her emails and checked her social media. Her American friends had posted some videos of a recent fashion show. It wouldn't play, so she called her husband.

'It's not the computer,' he said, 'it's the reception. It always gets worse in bad weather round here. All you can do is plug it directly into the router. Don't be long because I need it for work.'

The router was in the bedroom by the dressing table, so she had to put the computer in the middle of various gels and make-up sets. Once she had found a wide chair to place in front of the large oval mirror, she went online again. The videos played more clearly, and she watched them till she got bored. There was an open bottle of vermouth in the fridge, so she went downstairs and poured herself a glass.

'Are you eating yet?' she asked her husband. He shook his head. He still had work to do, so she put some pasta shells on to boil and poured a jar of spaghetti sauce into a pan, along with a whole packet of flaked ham. By the time the pasta had cooked, the vermouth was finished, and her husband had decamped to the bedroom. She went to look for the computer and then remembered it was upstairs. She had lost interest anyway. After the contents of the pans had been tipped onto a large plate and half a carton of double cream poured on top to cool it down, she had a good ten minutes worth of guzzling before it was all gone. She turned on the television and snored over a repeat of an afternoon soap. When that was finished, she slouched over the table. The day had been exhausting for her. She had just started to doze off again when her husband came pounding down the stairs.

'Damn,' he cried. 'I need all last year's contract summaries!' And he ran into his little study and began throwing open the filing cabinet drawers. 'Damn!' he called out again. 'Nothing is ever where it should be!'

'Who's fault is that?' she yelled back. But she couldn't relax in the kitchen with all his fussing and banging around.

'I'm going to bed,' she said. 'I've had enough for today.'

'Damn and blast it!' he said, rummaging through a cardboard box.

It wasn't unusual for her to go to bed early: she often got bored in the evenings and sitting at a screen for any length of time made her eyes sting. Also, although Ernest had failed to consume any champagne, she had succeeded with several refills, downing his as well. That, along with the vermouth still splashing around inside her, made her feel quite woozy. She decided to wait till the following day to email her American friends and tell them that she had seen the fashion show. She liked American fashion so much that she spent a great deal of money on designer wear. The fancy undergarments she bought gave her an affinity with the sylph-like models who paraded them on the New York catwalks, so even though they remained invisible to anyone other than Ernest, she had a regular supply on order.

She took off her top and thought of the afternoon she had spent with his work colleagues.

'Those idiots!' she yelled towards the open door. 'I never realised how ugly Peregrine's wife was.'

Her husband continued to rummage and bang about downstairs.

'Did you hear me?' she called again. 'And I don't how they manage to put up with Leverage. I've never heard such a whiney little fool in all my life.'

Her oversized breasts, which had once distracted her husband so terribly during their courtship, had begun their inexorable surrender to gravity even before she was halfway through her twenties, so she tended to avoid the mirror while she was undressing.

'And Basil!' she continued. 'I think it's a wonder he can show himself in daylight with that hideous great mark on his face! Disgusting!'

She struggled to get her pants off over her ankles since, being the size she was, standing on one leg for the necessary length of time to accomplish this routine took all her remaining dexterity (especially after the vermouth). As soon as she had succeeded, she passed wind noisily. After she managed to get back to a standing position, she twisted round intending to collapse onto the bed and switch off the light.

It was only then that she noticed the computer was still on. As her vision was still somewhat blurred from her alcoholic indulgence, she couldn't quite make out the fuzzy little squares that appeared and disappeared periodically on the computer that her stupid husband (as she assumed) had forgotten to turn off.

'You know this computer is still on!' she shouted, as she heard him slamming a door. 'I know it wasn't me because I remember switching it off after watching the fashion show.'

'I'm using it for work,' he said, clambering up the stairs. 'We're halfway through our first video conference.'

12. COME ON YOU FAIRIES!

'My dad's a wrestler!'

'So? My dad's a boxer!'

'Well, my dad's a pleesman!'

'My dad won the UEFA cup!' said the only girl in our group: eight-year-old Peony, the newest member of our little gang. However, the credibility of her declaration was somewhat compromised by her insistence on the presence of fairies in the woodland that adjoined our unmade road.

'No, he didn't.'

'Yes, he did. My mum said so.'

This provoked a great deal of scepticism, particularly on my part, but it was parried by Peony with such squeaky assertions that she managed to half convince the others. So against her wishes, we followed her past the large detached houses facing the forest and into the gloomy flats that stood squarely on the corner. She lived on the third floor.

Her mother invited us in with a smile. She was a stunning Canadian woman: tall, with mousy brown hair and mousy brown sunglasses to match. She offered us orange squash and confirmed her daughter's story. She also told us that the little girl had been christened Lisa, but her mother thought she took after the bright flower and named her so. I dedicate this story to both of them.

*****

'Mind out, why don't you?' The warning went unheard and unheeded because of the noise from the road drill that had been rumbling all morning. A car had driven too close to the workmen, and one of them, startled by its sudden proximity, lost his balance. The trench was only a two-footer, but he fell awkwardly.

The man who had given the warning jumped in after his colleague. The driver stopped, got out, and called down to the pair.

'Is he all right?'

'He's out cold.'

'He had his hard hat on though, didn't he? I'm so sorry, I didn't see the signs.' He eased himself down to the injured man, and several more workmen gathered around the edge.

'No, you didn't! That's a fact. You didn't see the signs that were up all over the place. We'll have to call 999.'

'I'm so sorry.'

'Look, he's coming to... Take it easy now... easy. Put your hands down. There's nothing there. Just relax, it's only air... That's it.'

'Is he breathing?'

'I think he's hallucinating.'

'Let's try and get him up. You'll have to help me, I can't lift him.'

*****

Light of step and fleet of foot through the late summer woodland they ran. The sun that glittered down through the trees was all the brighter for being intermittently obscured. It dappled the brown leaf mould and illuminated patterns in the bark. The earliest leaves of spring, still light in colour, glittered with the dew. Two children ran around the bushes, meeting and parting, the girl generally in front of the smaller boy. The woods came to an end where the private road made a T-junction with the public highway. Open wasteland was separated from the road by a ditch over which lay an old log. The boy hopped over.

'Wait, Perkin.'

Peony followed gracefully, and they walked safely across the unmade road that separated the houses from the trees. A block of flats, functional and bland, juxtaposed the wide houses and bungalows that ran the length of the hill.

'Here,' said Peony, going ahead of him. She ran up the path that led into the grounds of the flats.

'We're not allowed,' said Perkin.

'Scaredy-cat!'

He dashed after her, and they passed under an arch into a car park beneath the flats. At the far end, there was a narrow strip of lawn prolific with daisies and dandelions; next to it was a slant-roofed shelter where the waste bins were kept.

'See,' said Perkin. 'No fairies, you made it all up.'

Where the shelter joined the wall in front of the lawn, there was a small triangular gap. It was no bigger than the palm of a child's hand, and it could only be seen by kneeling down. Peony did so and held her forefinger in front of it.

'Shush,' she said.

The gap lit up with a violet glow.

'Ooh!' said Perkin as he collapsed next to her.

There was a buzz of soft wings, then a doll-like creature, no bigger than two thimbles, hovered over her hand; its blond hair billowing in the iridescence emanating from its body. Its tiny face was alabaster-white, and its nose was in a straight line with its forehead. For clothing, it wore a tunic made of two green leaves sewn together at the sides with slits where its wings protruded. The wings were as fine as white cotton, becoming invisible when they buzzed.

'I think they're flower fairies,' whispered Peony.

'Aww,' said her brother as it settled on her hand. He moved closer, and it darted back into the gap. He tried to reach in.

'No!' snapped Peony. 'You frightened her. Anyway, they only come to me.'

'I want to hold one.'

'Can't.' With that she stood up and walked out of the car park with Perkin reluctantly following.

'Remember your promise,' she said. 'You're not allowed to tell anyone.'

When she got to the log, she realised he wasn't following her. She turned round. He had gone back to the flats.

'Perkin!' She raced back and met him coming out. 'You can't go there without me. I'll tell if you do!' Perkin smirked and kept his hands firmly in his pockets.

As far as the promise went, Perkin seemed to be very good. Peony knew he hadn't said anything to their mother when she asked where they had been because she had stood behind the door and listened closely. When their mother agreed to let him have two of his friends from down the road over for an hour (if he promised not to make too much noise), Peony went and played in her room. Perkin never kept promises to not make any noise, so she was surprised when she heard nothing from downstairs. Nor were they in the garden when she looked out of the window. The mystery was solved when she heard her mother ushering the three boys out of the adjoining garage. After that, the two friends went home.

There were two playgrounds at their primary school: one for the upper two years and one for the lower three. Both were partially grassed and both had a concrete area with games, such as hopscotch, painted in bright colours. Peony was practising her skipping on the grass when one of Perkin's classmates strolled up and watched her.

'Go away,' she said. 'You're not allowed on this side.'

'Has Perkin really caught a fairy?' he asked. 'A real one?'

She stopped skipping.

The boy continued, 'Jimmy says he saw it in an upside-down fish tank.'

Peony was horrified. There used to be an old fish tank in the garage. Perkin had won a scrawny goldfish at the fair that appeared annually on the plains opposite the woods. Had he gone back and snatched a fairy from the gap in the wall? She was sickened by the thought.

'It's not real,' she said. 'It can't be!' She chased the boy away, then dashed into the lower playground to find her brother.

The lower school had a half-day on Thursdays, so when she couldn't find him in the last five minutes of the morning break, she was left with a full afternoon of awful speculation. When the bell went at 3pm, she dashed home as fast as she could and, without greeting her mother, ran straight through the house and out the back door. The garage was accessible from the garden by another door, but it was a squeeze even for her tiny form because her mother always parked the Cortina close to the wall.

There was a row of shelving on the far side where the detritus from various clean-ups had been dumped: toys that the children could not bear to throw out, old radios that still worked, tools that came with obscure kits, and some cigar boxes that had belonged to her granddad. To her relief, the fish tank was still there lying on its side. If he had done something horrible, as she suspected he might, then the fairy must have escaped. She examined its interior. There were some lilac marks, which she thought might be fairy dust, but there was also a lot of crusting from dried weed still stuck to it after it had been emptied at the end of the unfortunate fish's all-too-short life. She walked back into the house intending to confront Perkin and find out what he had done.

'Perkin,' she called as she walked into the kitchen, where her mother was preparing Angel Delight. Peony trotted into the adjoining dining room and stopped abruptly with her mouth open. A strange figure was sitting on the floor in front of her playing with Perkin's clockwork train. It had a large lantern jaw arching under ugly jowled cheeks that almost buried its beady little eyes. The head was too big for the body and its shoulders were too broad for its stringy arms. She was almost sick.

'What are you doing?' she gasped. The figure returned her gaze with something of a leer spreading on its thick grey lips.

'Ugh!' she cried, pointing. 'Mum, who's this? What's this?'

'Mum!' yelled the figure, its mouth making a big black "O".

'Peony, you must stop picking on your brother!'

'That ugly thing is not my brother!'

'Peony!'

The creature pointed a crusty finger back at her and burst into tears. Peony screamed, her mother shouted, and the creature howled like a mad wolf. The little girl dashed from the dining room through the kitchen, the hall, and out of the front door as her mother called after her, 'Peony!'

She darted through the gate and straight down the road. Her first thought was to go back to the flats, but there were several residents milling about outside. It was the time when the first of them returned from work, so she wandered tearfully onto the adjoining street, making her way aimlessly through its parked cars and terraced houses. She was so wrapped up in her predicament that she almost missed her Uncle Terry coming towards her. He was on his way to see her mother.

'What's all this?' he asked. 'Not crying, are you?'

'No,' she said. 'But I should be after what's happened. You've got to help me.'

He took her hand, and they walked up to the corner.

'You tell me what's happened,' he said. 'There's always an answer.'

'Come and sit on the log,' she said. They used to sit on that log when she was very young while Terry let his dog loose to play among the trees. Her uncle had always been a good listener, someone she could trust with her troubles.

'You know about fairies, don't you, Uncle Terry? Remember when I was young, you told me you'd seen them?'

He was smiling. She felt a little vexed.

'Uncle Terry, you told it me like it was true! Oh well, I can't talk to you after all.'

'It felt true at the time,' he said. 'I rerouted an entire gas pipeline because the fairies didn't want their entrance disturbed. Or so I thought. Go on. You tell me your fairy story.'

She started to explain, carefully watching his eyes for the tell-tale signs of incredulity. She saw none.

'Well,' he said when she had finished, 'it's quite clear to me that you've got a changeling.'

'What's one of those?'

'It's when they swap a human child for one of their own. Are you the only one who can see that it isn't your real brother?'

'Mum certainly can't. She honestly thinks it's Perkin!'

'That's usually the way. You see, you've got the fairy dust in your eyes.'

'That's all very well, but I have to get him back. I mean, I know he was a pain sometimes, but I can't have that awful creature in my house.'

'You'd better go and talk to the fairies. Tell them you want your brother back.'

'And will they give him to me?'

'I don't know,' her uncle replied. 'They might want something from you, or they might set you a task... or three.'

'I can't do tasks!'

Uncle Terry got up. 'Of course you can. Let's go, I want to see this changeling for myself.'

Back at the house they found the changeling crying over something else.

'I don't know what's the matter with Perkin today,' said her mother. 'Peony, have you upset him again?'

Peony looked at her uncle. 'See,' she said, 'Mum hasn't got a clue.'

'Blimey,' said her uncle. 'You'd better talk to those fairies as soon as you can before they get too used to having your brother with them in Fairyland.'

'Will they really give him back?'

Terry looked towards the kitchen where Perkin was having a tantrum. 'I'll tell you what, Peony, when you see them, mention me. I did help them out once. They'll probably remember.'

'I suppose I could do a task as well, if it's not too hard.'

'Ask to see the King.'

'Is that what you did?'

'No. He asked to see me!'

By seven o'clock, the cars were parked and the men, having returned from the city, were eating dinner in their flats. Peony's diminutive figure slipped unnoticed between the cars; she was all ears and eyes. A gold-coloured Cadillac was parked close to the metal bins, and she had to squeeze against it to get to the hole. She sighed and knelt as best as she could, dirt from the front grill rubbing onto her dungarees. No fairies. A few primroses had bloomed on the patch of grass. She examined them for fairy dust, but there was nothing brighter than the petals. The hole was just as dark as any hole in a brick wall might be. She moved her mouth up close to it, pursed her lips, and blew very gently.

Then she tilted her head back to look inside. Still dark. She blew again as softly as she could. Again nothing. She put both hands on the bricks and blew from above so her breath would take a downward trajectory. She blew long and softly, then slowly moved back. Darkness. Then, suddenly, a glimmer. She leaned back against the car, dirtying her top. The glow was like the reflection of daylight in a mirror. It flickered and faded slightly.

'Uncle Terry,' she whispered. 'He says he knows you. He helped you out once, he says.'

A man came out of the flats. She ducked down, her shoulder hard up against the black and white number plate of the Cadillac. He got into one of the cars. It wouldn't start first time. The grinding engine made a lot of noise, and sooty exhaust fumes drifted over to where she lay. It reversed painfully under the arch and abruptly came to a halt. She waited while it restarted and drove away, then she got up. The hole was dark once more. She sank back down to the ground, and as she put her hands back on the grass, she saw a fairy next to the primroses. She turned a hand over and eased her fingers in the direction of the flowers. The fairy hovered over the stalks and settled on her thumb. Peony raised it up. It turned its tiny face up towards hers. This one was dressed in a lilac jerkin and smart blue jacket. His black hair was swept back in a quiff, and he carried a golden wand in his tiny hands.

'Uncle Terry?' asked the fairy.

'Yes. He says you'll help me.'

'How?'

'I need to see the King,' she said. 'Can you take me?'

The fairy hopped up and circled over her palm. As it did so, fairy dust flew from its wand and wafted into the air. Then it beckoned with both hands and flew to the hole. Peony reached out and saw her arm was glittery with the dust; so was her other arm. To her surprise, she was glittering all over. The fairy had gone back into the hole, but now the light from it was brighter than before. Its miniscule arm came out and touched Peony's finger; then its hand gripped hers, and Peony found she had shrunk to the size of a playing card. The arch and the bins spun around her, and as the fairy pulled her into the void, she shrank even more.

What had once appeared to be no more than a dirty hole was now a delicately-carpeted passageway. Flaming torches hung on the walls and statues of heroes stood atop silver-railed pedestals. The fairy pulled Peony further in until they came to the end. A wrought twig gate with carefully-worked leaf and briar patterns across its width stopped them. Beyond the gate, she could see grassland and sky: a green, translucent sky with no sun but lots of little stars that shed enough light to give a clear view of the fields all the way to the horizon. The fairy waved his wand, the gate opened for them, and they passed softly through.

There were fairies everywhere. Apart from their dragonfly-thin wings, the fairies that went about their business could have been human beings like her. Some of them were weaving, some painting vases, and some skipping. A lot of them were earnestly throwing and kicking balls, making them spin so they bounced back towards them, and balancing them on their delicate feet. In one of the fields, she noticed what looked like a football match. She walked towards the action and saw that many of the players were wearing the white Spurs strip. Someone was shouting instructions, and the fairies were doing their best to follow, but as there were lots fairies and no one knew which ball belonged to whom, it was rather chaotic. Then she caught sight of who was giving the instructions.

'Perkin!' she called.

'Hey!' A voice came from behind. She turned and saw a creature, which by its gold robe, crown, and regal beard, she guessed was the King of the Fairies.

'Don't interrupt them.' he said. 'There's an important match coming up.'

Peony looked him up and down.

'Well,' he continued, 'I hear you wanted to see me?' His voice, though soft, had a rich baritone resonance as if he were speaking from across a canyon.

'Yes,' she said, pointing at Perkin. 'That's my brother. Can we have him back?'

'No.' said the King. He turned his back on her and walked towards the gate.

'Wait,' she called. 'You can't keep him. We need him. Can't you set me three tasks or something?' She ran after him.

'No,' he said, turning back to face her. 'We need him here. He's our top trainer. How do you expect us to win the league without a trainer?' He turned and walked away from her yet again.

'Stop,' she said. 'What do you mean "league"? Have you got a football league in Fairyland?'

He turned around and grinned at her. 'Not yet, but we will have.'

'And then what? How will you know about playing in a fairy league if you've never actually played in a real one? Perkin can tell you a few things about football, but he's only a little boy. He really can't help you very much.'

The King pulled on his beard. Four fairies flew up and settled in a square around him.

'Very well,' he said. 'Then you must help us in return for him. We need our team to play in the league. If you want your brother back, you must organise a match for us. We want to play Spurs. We'll have to play away though as our pitch isn't ready yet. If you can carry out that task, then you can have your brother back when he's finished training us.'

Each of the fairies took hold of a hand or a foot belonging to the King and lifted him up off the ground.

'But how?' cried Peony.

The King was whisked skyward by his four minions as fairy dust fell around her. 'Ask Uncle Terry!' he called.

Peony's original companion fairy took hold of her hand.

'This way,' he said in a lute-like voice. 'You have to go back now.'

'But what do I do? How can I carry out a task like that?'

The gate opened, and the fairy led her back down the passageway.

'Talk to your Uncle Terry,' he said, 'like the King said. Careful now, you're starting to expand.'

Peony leapt through the opening, just as she began to grow back to her proper size, and jumped lightly to the ground. She had to squeeze out from behind the Cadillac before she returned to her full dimensions as it had now been parked even closer to the hole.

On the far flanks of the forest, the Friday Hill Estate had been standing through the War and the London smog for some thirty years, yet it still looked new. The flint, which had been used to bulk out the concrete, glittered after the morning's short rainfall that had kept Peony indoors on the first few hours of her half-term holiday. The present sunshine saw her running over the railway bridge and up Simmons Lane where she met her Uncle Terry on his way to the betting shop.

'You know someone from Spurs, don't you!' she shouted breathlessly.

'Whoah! Hold your horses!' he replied. 'Slow down, won't you?'

'One of the players. I remember you told Perkin once.'

'Not a player,' said Terry. 'I've seen the manager, Bill Nicholson, around and about. I never said I knew him, but I know where he sometimes drinks.'

'Oh,' said Peony. 'I'm a bit cross then.'

'Why? What's with the sudden interest in football? I thought you preferred fairies.'

'There is a reason.'

Hatch Lane, tree-lined and open with a wide road and small local shops that did a thriving trade, meandered around the edge of the estate. At one time, it had boasted the best fish and chips in the country: an outlet called Hargreaves. Although long since closed, it had brought so much interest to the area that new money had settled there during the prosperity that followed rationing. At the same time, people like Peony's grandparents, who had been moved there during the slum demolition of the thirties, had made good of the change in their circumstances, and the Friday Hill Estate became the finest of its kind. In those days, there was only one betting shop, and its windows were blacked out so you couldn't see inside. No children were allowed in, so Terry left her outside with a bag of sweets for company.

'Terry! How are you, mate?' Terry was not surprised to see Nobby Clarke with a betting slip, nor was he surprised to see his long face.

'What's the matter, Nobs? You backed another donkey, mate?'

'Well,' said Nobby as he folded and unfolded a betting slip, 'I do have a good tip. If you could see me right for a bluey till Tuesday?'

'Now, now, Nobs. You don't want to get yourself in too deep, mate.'

'Come on, Tel. You know I'd do you a favour. I just need a few bob to tide me over.'

Terry reached into his trouser pocket where he always stuffed his banknotes. Nobby almost imperceptibly rubbed his ankles together.

'You can do me a favour too, Nobs. You're supposed to be good mates with Mr Nicholson, or so you keep telling us. Now as it happens, my little niece wants his autograph.'

Nobby rubbed his chin. 'I could sort that for you.'

'And she wants to meet him face-to-face to get it.'

Nobby straightened his back. 'Leave it out, Tel. I can't ask him that. He's a busy man.'

'Look at that: good odds on the 3 o'clock, I'd say. And there's a tenner in it for you.'

'Twenty.'

'Fifteen.'

'Twenty.'

'Seventeen!

'Nineteen!'

'Blimey, Nobs! He's not royalty!'

'He is if you're a Spurs fan.'

Terry left before the next race because he couldn't keep the girl outside any longer and because he didn't want to see Nobby's face when he lost all his money. He'd seen that face too many times before.

'Saturday,' he said to her. 'You'll 'ave to ask your mum because we might be back late, but I've sorted it for seeing Bill.'

Persuading her mother wasn't easy.

'I'm not sure I really want my daughter wandering around Enfield on a Saturday night,' she said.

Terry sipped his tea. 'It isn't that far: three stops on the tube. It's just the other side of the River Lea.'

'So long as she doesn't end up in it!'

'I'll see she's all right, love.'

She grimaced. 'I'll hold you to that. And it mustn't be too late.'

This arrangement gave Peony a week to see the fairies and tell them of her plans. Her fairy guide, he of the golden wand, was called Tatterdemalion, an enthusiastic player himself.

'You need to keep the ball nearer your feet when you dribble,' she told him, 'and don't lean forward so much.'

'Good, good,' said the little King. 'I want you to inspect our team while you're here.'

A silver coach in the shape of a walnut pulled by four seahorses floated down next to her, and she stepped inside.

'Hello, Perkin,' she called, arriving at the pitch.

'What's she doing here?' he scowled.

She got out, and the coach sped skyward. The fairy players had sensibly adopted a lilac strip: quite distinct from the white of the Spurs team. While Perkin glumly ignored her, she took one of the balls and kicked it into the goal from the penalty spot. None of them could prevent it going in.

'Next piece of advice: only use one football at a time.'

'I've been saying that for ages!' moaned Perkin. 'They don't listen.'

'In Fairyland, things can be backwards,' said the King. 'You should tell them to use lots of footballs, and then they will use just one.'

Peony took another shot and scored again. 'Right,' she said, 'goalkeeping. Watch me. Perkin, take a shot.'

He did so, and she stopped it with her feet. He came into the penalty area to try to tackle her, and she kicked the ball between his legs. The fairies cheered, and Perkin went off to sulk.

'That,' she said, 'is called a nutmeg. Now, gather round me.'

As soon as she told them about Bill Nicholson, they all wanted to meet him, having heard Perkin's eulogies on his god-like status among the fans. She told them it wasn't possible for them all to meet him, but...

Saturday afternoon saw Peony and her uncle on the train to Walthamstow Central where they caught the underground to Tottenham Hale. It was a short bus ride to Northumberland Park, and they sat upstairs so Peony could look out of the window. It stopped almost exactly outside the pub, and they had to push through a crowd on the pavement to get in.

'Kids are only allowed in this part,' said Terry, 'and your mum wants you back by 9:30pm, so we have to hope he's there.'

'She said 10:00pm to me.'

They cautiously went through the door. Terry nodded at the barman who was serving. He nodded back and indicated a table where the pair could sit. Then Terry saw Nobby. 'Come on,' he said, and they moved towards him. Nobby was wearing a long coat; he wasn't carrying a drink.

'Here, Tel,' he said, 'I'm a bit embarrassed. I got let down badly on that tip.'

'Now, Nobby…'

'If you could see your way to a bluey, mate, so we can sit down with Bill.'

Terry grinned. 'So he's here then?'

'Yeah, yeah, mate. A bluey. Cheers, Tel. Tuesday. No, Monday. Come on.'

'All right, all right, just as soon as we get the goods.'

Nobby led them to a table where Bill Nicholson sat with a few pals around him.

'What's a bluey?' asked Peony. 'And why does Nobby like them, Uncle Terry?'

Bill Nicholson looked up.

'A couple of fans,' said Nobby. 'Is that all right?'

'Has to be, doesn't it? How much did they pay you then?'

'Now, Bill!'

Peony leaned forward on the table and stared straight at him. He was older than she expected. Older even than Uncle Terry.

'Bill Nicholson?' she asked.

'Yes, that's me.' Bill leant on his elbows.

'I've got a proposition for you.'

One of the others at the table sniggered, 'Your lucky day, ain't it?'

'I don't do propositions on a Saturday night.'

'It's about the team,' she said seriously.

'Then I really don't do propositions on a Saturday night.'

'It'll only take five minutes.'

Terry put his arm round her. 'Peony, you must remember Bill is a busy man.'

'Peony…' said Bill, 'That's your name, is it?'

'Yes, it's a kind of flower. Five minutes, please, Bill?'

'And then you'll go?'

Nobby's face grew urgent. 'Before you go, Tel,' he said, rubbing his thumb against his fingers.

'Nobby wants a bluey,' said Peony by way of explanation. They laughed and ribbed him, but Peony remained serious. 'It's private,' she said.

'You know what,' said Bill generally to the table, 'you try to come out for a quiet drink and you get all this. Right, you two, in here, and you get five minutes.'

He led them past the kitchen and the toilets into a small conference room, where a round wooden table and a few chairs could accommodate a quiet discussion better than a noisy pub lounge. They sat down in a business-like fashion, and Peony placed a closed fist as far as she could reach onto the middle of the table.

'There is a new football team in Fairyland and they want to play Spurs.'

'Fairyland,' growled Bill, regarding Terry with suspicion.

'Yes,' replied Peony.

Terry got the brunt of Bill's annoyance.

'And you're in on this fairy stuff, are you? What sort of…'

Peony opened her fist, and the green-winged jerkin-clad Tatterdemalion danced across the table.

'Blimey!' said Terry.

'Very clever, I do not think,' snapped Bill.

The little creature somersaulted gracefully and threw fairy dust at them.

'I don't expect to see you two or your toys in here again,' said Bill standing up. Tatterdemalion flew up onto his shoulder. Bill tried to bash him, and he flew over his head.

'What's the deal, Bill?' squeaked the fairy.

'Whaa… aah!' Bill twisted around, trying to chase it and escape at the same time. It threw more dust around.

'Blimey!' said Terry, falling backwards off his chair. Bill pirouetted wildly as the fairy flew round and round his head. Terry righted himself and backed into the furthest corner, but dizzy from spinning this way and that, Bill tumbled. Tatterdemalion dived and grabbed the shoulder of his jacket. One of the greatest managers in the history of English football was then plumped unceremoniously into a chair by a tiny fairy. He took a minute to get his breath back. Peony chaired the ensuing proceedings with her arms neatly folded.

The bus back to the station was very crowded, so Peony and Terry had to stand for the short ride. When they got off Terry spoke. 'I don't think it's wise to make deals with them.'

'With the fairies?' said Peony. 'I thought you knew all about them. You always said you did.'

'Yes, but… I didn't know they were, well…'

'Small? Had wings? Flew around?'

'Well…'

'Cast magic spells?' She narrowed her eyes and spun an invisible thread with her fingers.

'I think you should be very careful.'

'What about Perkin?'

'I'm saying nothing.'

'You'll have to say something. He might want you in the team next week! Remember Perkin is their coach. The real Perkin, I mean. Anyway, what happened to you when you were with them?'

They made their way down to the Underground and had to sit in a full carriage, so it wasn't until they got to the platform at Walthamstow that Terry was able to tell his story.

'I think your little fellow was there too when I saw them.'

'So now you know you did see them.'

'They didn't want the trench to go quite where we were digging it, and they made me agree to alter the plans.'

'So, you did.'

'I wouldn't have got out if I hadn't. I've never been quite sure if I'd dreamed it or not. Not till just now. Blimey.'

The train was on time, and it took just under half an hour to get home. Terry was invited in for a cup of tea. The changeling had got hold of a can of lager and was making himself sick.

'I told you, Mum,' she said. 'It's not really Perkin.'

'You really aren't helping,' she replied. 'I just wish you'd stop saying that, especially to him!'

Peony rolled her eyes, and her uncle diplomatically left.

The White Hart Lane Priority Passes came in the post the following Monday. The following Thursday saw Peony and her uncle embark on another train journey. It was a sunny evening, and she wore a light coat. By the time they changed onto the Underground at Walthamstow, it was positively warm. It took about half an hour to walk to the ground from Seven Sisters Station, and Peony held her uncle's hand tightly. The sun shone brightly on the colourful clothing of the moving crowds. The stadium stood tall and impressive before them. Bill had sent a map with directions to a special turnstile round the side. The man who took and perused their passes led them to the new South Stand.

'I don't know what's going on here tonight,' he said as he led them up the stairs. 'There's no youth team matches and most of the maintenance lot have been given a holiday. Something's up, but I don't know what.'

They trotted onwards to the front row without answering him.

The turnstile man looked at his watch. 'Nearly 5:30 and no sign of anything happening. This might be a waste of time.'

'Might be,' said Terry.

'I spoke to Jimmy Neighbour this morning. He's a mate of mine. He coaches my kids at school. He reckons it's Russians.'

'It might be.'

Peony grinned at her uncle as the man walked off.

'Russian fairies!' she said.

It was strange to be alone in such a huge space, especially as a white mist was beginning to descend. Peony shuddered.

'Should have wrapped up more,' her uncle remonstrated. 'It can get very cold at matches. It does at Arsenal.'

'Where are they?' asked Peony. 'Is anything happening?'

'If anything does happen, we may not be able to see it anyway,' he replied. 'This fog is getting thicker by the minute.'

The mist, creamy white and velvety on the tongue, rolled over and around them until they couldn't even see the clock opposite. It grew very cold.

'Look!' cried Peony, pointing to where the further goal would have been if they could see it. There was a lilac light flickering in the whiteness. The edge of it became tinged with green, and it grew brighter as the fog began to clear.

'Blimey!' said Uncle Terry.

'At last,' said Peony. 'I think it's all going to happen like they said.'

Suddenly, they noticed they weren't alone. The whole stand was filled with forms and figures of all shapes, sizes and colours.

'They've grown bigger,' she said.

'I s'pose they'd have to if they were going to play football,' said Terry.

The assortment on the pitch was even stranger. Thin and fat, tall and short, feathered and winged, young and very, very old. A wizened, bent-up creature led them to the mid-field. Silence fell. They waited. There was a rumble. Voices. Then the Spurs team, led by Martin Peters, emerged from the tunnel. He raised his arm and hailed the opposing team. Then he looked up. The sky was completely obscured by a dome of bright white fog. This allowed Peony and her uncle to see the pitch without difficulty. They watched the wizened figure make his way toward Martin Peters.

'I reckon he's the ref,' said Terry.

The Spurs team cautiously made their way to midfield.

'There's Tatterdemalion!' shouted Peony. 'He must be their captain.'

The Spurs team saw the fairies, looked at each other, then headed back to the tunnel.

'No!' cried Peony.

'Noooo!' cried the Green Children of Suffolk from behind them.

'Ohhhhh!' wailed the Three Weeping Widows of Abingdon.

A figure in black strode onto the pitch. It was Bill Nicholson. He called Martin Peters, and the referee hurried towards him. The First Division footballers formed a huddle with him while the ref remonstrated.

'The manager isn't allowed on the pitch,' explained Terry.

Bill walked towards the stand, and the teams approached the mid field. Tatterdemalion shook hands with Martin and produced a huge hazelnut. He placed it on the centre spot.

The ancient referee took out his whistle. The sound was low and strained, as though it had come from mountains of ice. Tatterdemalion took out a mallet from inside his brown cloak and cracked open the nut. It exploded loudly, and a ball flew into the air. Some sylphs and little Fairy Forget-Me-Not flew after it. Pat Jennings ran back to the Spurs' goal while Cyril Knowles and Steve Perryman took up positions near the box. The sylphs took the ball in mid-air and passed it to Forget-Me-Not, who brought it to the ground. As soon as it landed, an ugly red-cap snatched it and hurtled toward the Spurs goal. From where she sat, Peony could see the twist on the misshapen creature's face, even his own players avoided him. Chivers raised his hands and looked at the referee, who shrugged. As Cyril Knowles moved out of the way to let him pass, it looked as though it was just Red-Cap and Jennings. Red-Cap had the ball for a moment when Terry Naylor suddenly barged into him and kicked it away. It flew up before coming down in front of him. Naylor dandled it between his feet as the monster howled and ran at him, but he was met with a shoulder and tumbled to the ground raising a hand toward the ref. Naylor booted it and yelled, 'Gilzean!'

'Blimey!' said Terry.

'Ooh! Ooh!' whispered the North and South Winds from the back of the stand. The Weeping Widows raised a scarf above their heads, which the Winds gently filled out.

Alan Gilzean took possession of the ball and dribbled it toward the fairy goal, but he was overtaken by Fairy Marigold whose beautiful gold wings momentarily dazzled him. Marigold dived down and headed the ball up from the ground, but Alan leapt into the air, and with the grace of a rattlesnake, arced his body to produce a header that sent the ball straight into the fairy goal. One-nil!

One of two yellow fauns was chosen to take the centre. He booted it to Tatterdemalion who, discovering Naylor running toward him, quickly passed it to the red-cap. Martin

Peters tried to tackle him from behind, but Jilly Trinket wound into him and took the ball in her pale green cloak. Naylor cried "foul", but the ref ignored him. Neighbour was there in an instant and kicked the ball through the soft material. It went straight towards an unmarked player, John Pratt, but in passing it to Peters, he tripped and fell over it. Naylor swore, and Peters put his hands over his face.

'I can't believe Nicholson,' said Terry. 'He sold Souness and kept Pratt!'

Pratt was up, but Red-Cap had already taken the ball from him and sent it down the pitch. Two hobgoblins received it and played it between each other as Naylor went for each in turn. Then Red-Cap barged into him, and he went down with a bump. The decayed ref blew his low whistle as Naylor lay there. A penalty was awarded to the fairies. The Spurs team could not believe the injustice. Naylor was up in a shot and strode towards the ref.

'Easy, Terry,' said Peters, catching up with him. 'Terry, I mean it.'

Peony looked at her uncle. 'I don't know much about football,' she said, 'but I know that was wrong. The fairies fouled our player, so why do they get the penalty.'

'The ref forgot his glasses,' he replied.

'Oh,' she said. 'So that's why then.'

Red-Cap took the penalty, and it went in because Jilly Trinket had cast her cloak over Jennings. He threw it off and, seeing the ball in the goal, shouted something at the referee. The ref held up a yellow card. Jennings looked at Peters and snorted with contempt.

Cyril Knowles took the centre and kicked it toward Chivers who ran forward and took it, despite an attempt by the hobgoblins to trip him up.

'On the 'ead!' he yelled, sending it in the air to Neighbour who headed it toward Gilzean. Gilzean had an open goal and would have easily booted it in, but Marigold got to it first by flying over the top of them. She kept it up for a few moments, and then let it go to a gentle nod from Forget-Me-Not. The ball went back and forth: sometimes in the air, sometimes swiftly along the grass, and sometimes turning into a turnip. At half-time, they changed ends, but neither side managed to get a decent shot at a goal. Then, as Forget-Me-Not flew past Naylor taking the ball into the air for the umpteenth time, Naylor grabbed her ankles and swung her to the ground. Forget-Me-Not vanished in a puff of pink smoke. The fairies' supporters wailed and howled, and Terry Naylor raised his hands. It was a red card. Both teams were now a player down. Bill Nicholson talked to the ref.

'What's happening?' asked Peony.

'I don't think Spurs have got a sub,' said Terry.

'Have the fairies?'

There was an argument going on between the referee and Nicholson, which the latter by the manner of his retreat, appeared to have lost. The ball was placed on the spot where Forget-Me-Not had vanished, and the fairies all stood back. They did have a substitute. In full gear (boots, shorts, and lilac top), he ran on and took the penalty with power. It was her brother, Perkin! The ball sailed through the air and went straight past Jennings, who, though unimpeded by fairy mischief, failed to stop the goal. The referee blew his whistle, long and low. The fairies all hugged and jumped on each other's backs.

'What's that all about?' shouted Uncle Terry.

'It's time,' said the nearest Widow.

'No it ain't. Its only 5:30!'

'Look!' All three widows pointed up. Slowly and almost imperceptibly, the mist was starting to swirl around. Nicholson was on the pitch. His hands were on his hips, and he was shaking his head. Perkin was doing a headstand, and the Spurs players were leaving. The fairy supporters were fading away, and the mist was getting colder. Peony and Terry walked down towards the pitch. They clambered over the barrier to find Nicholson talking to Tatterdemalion.

'Always remember, Bill,' he said, 'it's better to keep your targets high and fail than to succeed with low aims.'

Marigold fluttered above them excitedly. 'Red-Cap has been named Fairy of the Match!' she said, clapping her hands.

The mist swirled around them making Peony shiver. It was getting harder and harder to make out the fairy footballers, but she could hear them gently shrieking.

'Where's Perkin?' she asked. 'Do we get him back now?'

'Yes,' said Tatterdemalion. 'And we get our changeling back.'

Bill Nicholson grunted. 'What do we get out of this, apart from useless homilies?'

Tatterdemalion waved his wand and spread fairy dust on the grass around them. 'Luck,' he answered.

He didn't specify what kind of luck, and within a year Nicholson was gone, and Spurs had gone down to the Second Division. Never trust a fairy.

As far as her brother was concerned, Tatterdemalion was as good as his word. Perkin returned, and, although as irritating as before, he was never as weakly as the changeling. She saw no more of the fairies after that, although she did read about some suspicious sightings in Walthamstow when an old gas main was replaced.

Years passed. Peony did not take any further interest in football until she had two little boys of her own. Her young husband took them to White Hart Lane as soon as they could walk, and she would watch the matches live on television to see if she could spot them in the crowd. There was usually a magazine or some knitting in front of her because she still didn't really understand the game and couldn't tell one player from another, despite her husband's enthusiastic descriptions.

Once, however, she did spot a particularly quick performer. It was during a match against Arsenal, their greatest rivals, when she noticed the Number 8 shirt having trouble with his boots. There was something familiar about him that she couldn't quite put her finger on. When he twisted round the goalkeeper and scored wearing just one sock, she started out of her seat: the lantern jaw, the beady eyes, the broad shoulders, and those stringy arms.

'And the first goal,' pronounced the commentator, 'was scored by their new centre forward..."

13. CHEAP FRILLS

'And I'll tell you one thing,' said Des, who had more "one things" to say than we could remember over his years of shifting gear in the markets and bars of North Devon. It was never "one thing", but a pile of anecdotes and examples that he believed demonstrated a rationalised tolerance, unblemished by liberal education or political correctness, and which were always accompanied by a straight forefinger aimed at the dolts and fashions born of the present times. He wasn't a small man and he wasn't a big man. He wasn't mean with money, but he wouldn't be taken for a fool by anyone. Clean-shaven, with a head of thick black hair that kept its colour until his middle sixties, he would often hold his full pint glass aloft as though it were a trophy won for his insight into the nature of this country's downfall.

There were limits. There were lines to be drawn. That these lines did not always tally with the law of the land was fair enough, as he assured us in brash terms. He liked buying and selling; he respected the elderly; and he drove an old Volkswagen. It wasn't easy to argue with him, but he was good value after a few pints if he could be inveigled into contradicting something he had said on a previous night. That was when the finger started wagging. It was his stock-in-trade tic. The more flustered he got, the wider the range of its wag.

Des primarily worked in the local markets. He took his regular slots in Barnstaple and South Molton, but whenever there were opportunities for richer pickings, he would go to Bideford or Ilfracombe. He rarely travelled out of Devon.

He specialised in small items of clothing and general knick-knacks for women. In his later years, he turned to saris and kimonos to meet the changing demographic. He would always tell us how beautiful the Asian women looked, especially when they wore clothing that he had sold them. His suppliers had bases all over the country, and he boasted that there wasn't much he couldn't get hold of. Occasionally, he would display video tapes at the front of the trestle table, and, for those "in the know", other videos could be found in one of the boxes stashed underneath. Much of his gear came from warehouses that had overstocked or businesses that had gone bankrupt (this was in the days before Matalan and TK Max), but there was also a fair proportion that hadn't come through Customs and Excise. Some of the designer labels were labels only, but Des kept that little game to a minimum, having nearly had his fingers burned once. Nevertheless, it was a good living, and he loved the bonhomie of the community. He owned a house that backed onto a river where he could fish. Fishing was his passion, and he planned to do a lot of it when he retired.

'I've worked all my life,' said Des, his finger jabbing the air. 'So no one is telling me I can't enjoy my retirement.' Nobody was. He was going to sell up his stall and its name, his list of suppliers (the legitimate ones), and all with the last of his stock. He had recently considered several offers, and, as he told us, it was a case of "strike while the iron's hot". His only problem was the tax situation.

In the old days, it was simply a case of filling in a few forms and making a bit of an estimate (his would always be favourable to himself), then sending it to an accountant. However, as he himself said, since self-assessment had been brought in, he hadn't really got around to it. Eventually, four jolly years had passed.

The best advice we could give was: "Des, you're going to have to do something if you're selling up or they'll just come after you." So-and-so knew someone who had lost their house, and someone else had a mate who was doing time. "You really should have acted a bit sooner, mate" was the least helpful. He knew that eventually he would have to square things up.

'I'll go in Monday,' he said.

And one Monday, he did.

The Barnstaple Tax Office was behind the bus station, a little way past the Post Office sorting depot. It was a red-brick building with a wide entrance consisting of two reinforced glass doors: one of which was held open by a wall hook and catch. Des parked in the council car park opposite the police station. He put an hour on the ticket, but he didn't think it would take that long to get the advice he wanted. He stepped through the doors, looked down the corridor and up the stairs. There was a sign that said "Tax Office" and the start of a red guide-line (amongst other coloured lines that led to different civic functions). He followed it with his eyes. It led upstairs.

'Can I help you?'

A pleasant-looking woman with straight, brown hair tied back in a bun and wearing a smart business suit had approached him from the side.

'Yes, I'm looking for some advice on my tax situation,' he said. If he had seen her in the market, he might have held up a light-blue blouse to match the colour of her eyes.

'That's my department. I can see you right now if you have time. Would you like to come upstairs?'

Of course he wouldn't "like to". No one likes paying their taxes, but he steeled himself and followed her into an open-plan office.

'Can I take your name?' she asked as they settled into opposing chairs.

'I'm Des. Desmond Meacher. And you?'

'Call me Chris.'

'Short for Christine?'

'No, Christabel. Your enquiry is…?'

Des shuffled awkwardly. 'Yes, it's my self-assessment. I've been having a bit of trouble with it.'

'We can help out, within reason. If you can give us all the information, we can have a proper interview to help you put it all together.'

'This was easy,' thought Des. He felt more confident.

'I work on the markets, you see. And with me, it's suppliers, and outgoings, and cash flow problems, so…'

'That's all right,' she smiled kindly. 'It's all self-explanatory on the forms. If you have everything written down somewhere, we can show you where it goes.'

'And it goes back a bit.'

'How far does it go back?' She was still smiling, though the ends of the smile were becoming rather static.

'Oh, a couple of years or so.' Rolling his head towards the interesting ceiling patterns, he didn't notice that she was no longer smiling.

'How many years?'

'Four.'

'Are you saying you've avoided paying any tax for four years?'

It was then that he noticed her expression had changed.

'It's this self-assessment thing. I couldn't get the hang of it, you see. I'm an old man. I want to retire, so I want to sort it out. That's why I'm here.'

Supporting herself with the arms of the chair, she re-adjusted her position and sat further forward.

'Well, I'm glad you've come to us now. We'll do what we can, but you must appreciate there will probably be a penalty involved. You see, even if you aren't eligible to pay tax for whatever reason, you still have to declare your earnings.'

Des knew enough about tax and the law not to plead ignorance of the fact. She made an appointment for an interview that left him enough time to collect all his invoices together: the ones going back over four years. He left the office with his shoulders hunched and his head down.

We weren't much use to him in The Plough Inn that night. The best advice we could give was to be as straightforward as possible. It didn't sound as though the fine would be extortionate from what he had said, but then what did we know?

'The only two certainties in life are death and taxes,' said Gerry the landlord, placing his elbows on the bar. 'They always get you in the end. I remember a mate of mine losing absolutely everything.'

'It's only been four years,' said Des. 'I haven't robbed a bank or anything. You get all these people living off the welfare state, and I've never claimed for anything. It's ridiculous, if you ask me.' Out came the finger. 'I've never asked anyone for anything. Not like some people. I'll tell you one thing: the whole world's gone mad. That's what's happened. Everything I've got, I've worked for, and now they're going to take my house off me.'

Gerry raised his palms in a gesture of calm. 'No one said that you'll lose your house, Des. All you've got to do is go in, stay calm, and put your hands up to it. You made an error of judgement, that's all.'

'I'll tell you one thing,' he wagged, 'if I'm going to be fined, and my fine is going to those people who make a profession of living off the state, then I'm only declaring what I have to.'

We thought he was only going to do that anyway.

'No,' he put us right on that. 'I've always paid my taxes. I'm proud to support my country, you know, the military and the police, but if they're going to pick on me when I've worked all my life, then I'll tell you one thing…'

Gerry brought his right ear as close to his shoulder as was necessary to impress upon Des a sincere concern for his recklessness whilst simultaneously remaining sympathetic to his predicament.

'Des,' he said, 'you be careful. They aren't stupid. If they see you've been putting money in the bank or going on holiday, they will come after you. And it might not be now, it might be in a few years time.'

But Des was not going to be subdued.

'An Englishman's home is his castle!' he declared, holding his pint aloft.

Gerry shook his head. 'There are only two things in this life that we can be certain of,' he said. 'One is death, the other is taxes.'

Des was never gloomy for long. Over the following days, he collated all his assets and cobbled together as many of his records as he could. Where he had to "redo" them, so to speak, the figures fell to his pecuniary advantage.

The day of the interview came. Des parked in the council car park and retrieved his box of invoices and receipts from the back seat. Carefully balancing it on his knee and placing his foot on the tyre, he fumbled for his key and nearly fell over. When you get to seventy, it's harder to perform such acts of contortion. The trouble is, at that age, you also forget that they have become harder, as Des could tell us. He put the box on the roof of the car, locked the driver's door, and with the keys still in his hand, took out his self-assessment form and rested it on top of the box. Then he went to the ticket machine, came back to the car, put the ticket on the windscreen, locked up, retrieved the box, and pushed the form inside without opening it again. Then he stood still and got his breath back.

Arriving at the building, he found Christabel standing in the stairwell in front of the sign displaying the list of official departments. She was speaking in clipped tones to a couple of young men. The attitude of her audience suggested that it wasn't something they particularly wanted to hear. He noticed that her hair was wound more tightly into its bun than it had been on his last visit and that her shoes were larger and less suited to her dress. Perhaps her eyes weren't blue after all. It was hard to tell when they were so narrowed. Maybe that light-blue blouse would not have been such a good idea, he conjectured.

'Mr Meacher, isn't it?'

Realising that they were no longer the focus of her attention, the two men slipped away.

'We're quite short-staffed today,' she said. 'In here, please.'

He was led into a small room with a sloped ceiling on the ground floor. Seated under its lowest point, it seemed as though all the energy therein was directed towards him. He took out his self-assessment form and showed her how he had filled it in as best as he could. She nodded gravely as he opened the pages and pointed out the parts he had found difficult.

'Is this everything?' she asked. 'Obviously you deal with a lot of cash in hand in the market trade. We realise that.'

'I think this is all,' he lied.

'It needs to be absolutely complete before it's submitted, so if we have any questions, we'll get back to you sooner rather than later.'

She fixed him with her gaze. He quailed as he remembered Gerry's words in the pub. A lot of his trade was cash in hand, and he had been on several good holidays in the last few booming years. Perhaps he should have owned up to a bit more.

'There is the question of the last three years,' she added. 'We'll reach a decision on that when everything has been processed.'

Des thought about saying something there and then, but he couldn't think exactly what he should say, so gave up.

'We'll need to refer to this,' she pointed at the box. 'If you can leave it here for a week or so, we can deal with your case.'

He had a case. That sounded ominous. He swallowed hard and rose from his seat, feeling the need to breathe fresh air.

'Wait a minute,' she said, 'I'll get you a receipt.'

She went out of the door, and he heard her tap-tapping down the corridor. Remembering an invoice that represented an area of the economy he felt would be best kept under wraps, he eased the box towards him. Too late! Footsteps indicated her proximity, and she burst in waving a signed receipt.

His route back across town was as dismal as before. As he reached his car, a police van pulled out onto the road, and he gulped involuntarily. He felt in his pocket for his keys. They weren't where he expected them to be. Nor were they where he didn't. He thumped the front window. Of course! He had left them in the box with all his receipts and records. He kicked the front wheel.

He did a quick calculation. It should have taken him less than ten minutes to get to the tax office, but he reckoned that, carrying the box, it had taken him just over fifteen. The meeting had been long enough for him to estimate he had about twenty minutes left on his hour's ticket, but now he had to get there and back again. This simple maths meant he would probably end up with a parking ticket to top off his awful day. He swore angrily and stomped out of the car park.

Inside the building, he saw people rushing up and down the stairs and back and forth along the corridor. They looked stressed. Then he remembered hearing someone say that they were short-staffed. It wasn't going to be easy to find his box.

The room where the interview had taken place was locked, so he followed the red line upstairs to the tax office to see if he could track down Christabel. As he reached the top of the stairs, he happened to glance into a side alcove stacked with papers and boxes. He let his eyes drift down the rows of shelves, and, joy of joys, there was his box! The two men Christabel had been talking to earlier came up the stairs, so he turned his back to them while they entered the tax office. Stopping just inside the room, they began to hold an earnest conversation.

He picked up the box and inched toward the stairs, fiddling with its folded lid. Suddenly, the men reappeared. Still holding his box, he turned and quick-stepped down the stairs in front of them. As he reached the bottom, he heard Christabel's voice droning along corridor. He hesitated briefly in the stairwell. At this rate, he, Christabel, and the two men were all on collision course to meet by the entrance doors. Not wanting to explain why he had the box in his arms, he ran outside and hid around the corner. He could have opened the box and retrieved his keys, and maybe that awkward little invoice, but there were only ten minutes left on the car park ticket. So with a new momentum in his step and a new consideration whirling in his brain, he headed for the car. After quickly retrieving his keys, he shoved the box into the boot and drove home.

A few days later, he got the phone call he was expecting from an effusively apologetic Christabel.

'I am so sorry. We don't know how it happened. We're usually so careful.'

Des was ready for her. He had even written out his spiel on a notepad. 'But that's got all my suppliers! How do I know what I'm owed or when I'm supposed to pay them? And then there's all my contacts and records! What am I going to do? This could ruin me!'

'It is most regrettable. However, we do ask that people make copies of all of their accounts.'

'But I didn't know you wanted to keep it, and you know how much there was in there. It would've taken ages to make copies of it all. No! No! No! It's not good enough!'

Des related his little anecdote many times in The Plough. Perhaps a few details changed over the years, but suffice to say, his tax bill was risibly small, and the fine was next to nothing. This was his getting even with "all those people who live off the state". Des entered retirement in his seventieth year, and I am delighted to say it was a most enjoyable one for him.

*****

By including himself in this narrative, the author makes an exception. In doing so, he must add, for the sake of any members of Her Majesty's noble squadron of revenue collectors who might like to catch up with Des, that they undoubtedly will: since he is now in the place that, according to our mortal state, remains, along with taxes, equally certain.

14. LAURA'S LAST ORCHID

Look after your prisoners. That's the sign of a civilised society. We become what we do, so let them tend flowers. Let them tend flowers, and they will learn to bring beauty into existence. Take Scannie Scanlon: thirty years for homicide, but he's never going to get out. If he ever comes up for parole, there will be a big media splash, and no government wants to be seen as the one that set Scannie Scanlon free. It's all a bit rich really. There are plenty of others who've done far worse that you don't hear about, and they're walking around free.

'Blow on them, Martin. Don't put them straight into the pots dry.'

Martin Puzzle: aggravated burglary and several counts of manslaughter. Now, he probably will get out, but he's not thinking about that at the moment. He's growing orchids. He loves it. See, Martin's never really experienced anything beautiful in his life. As a place to grow up, Hackney wasn't that pretty in the '70s. Then he got in with the wrong crowd, and the sort of things they did to old ladies wasn't at all pleasant. So it was lucky for him that he fell in with Scannie, because everybody knows Scannie, and he's all right really.

'Like this, Martin. From the bottom of your lungs,' Scannie said.

He held the seeds in his cupped hands. As he softly made his wet breath pass through them, his slender build, bony shoulders, and thin sandy hair came together to create the appearance of an angel in the glass of the greenhouse.

'See now?'

He did it a couple more times till he saw the seeds change colour in the wet of his warm breath. He dripped them from the gap between his smallest fingers, making them fall separately into a two centimetre-wide trench marked out in a long box.

'They'll all germinate now,' he said. They probably would too. *Orchis dextiphilliac* was the rarest of the species for a very good reason: it was almost impossible to grow outside its fast-disappearing natural habitat.

The Green Earth Trust had laid out the prison allotments in strips: not unlike the open-field system of medieval Europe. Each strip had a greenhouse at one end. Prisoners were free to decide on its use within the rules laid down by the Biodiversity Commission. The time prisoners were allowed to spend there was not only relative to good behaviour, but also to outcome. In preserving rare species of orchid, no one was more valuable to the Trust than Scannie.

When a man reaches a certain age, things don't come as easy, so Scannie was passing his skills on to his cellmate, Martin. Although Martin could sometimes be volatile, he was a quick learner, and more importantly, he trusted Scannie. The apprentice was doing well, as long as they didn't wave the old parole thing in front of him.

'Like this, Scannie?'

Martin blew too hard, making the seeds fly about.

'Gently now! Don't lose them!'

It was a secret knack that was easy to pick up, but he couldn't remember if it was something he had discovered accidently or intuitively. It always worked with orchids, especially the more delicate ones. But Martin would soon get it. He was all right, really, was Martin.

*****

Prison food was never up to much. Well, I suppose it depends on what you like. You get your bit of meat and your bit of greens, but it was all a bit stodgy. Mind you, some of the lads liked it like that.

'I'll have yours, Martin!' said Podgy Wilson.

'Sure. You can have my food,' said Puzzle. 'And you can have my fist for dessert.'

Scannie fixed his eyes on Wilson. 'Maybe if you didn't eat your dinner quite so quickly, you might enjoy it for longer.'

They all laughed at the idea of enjoying dinner, but Scannie didn't take his eyes off Wilson till Evans piped in.

'I mean, all right and all that, but how come Puzzle gets to go off-site after everything. That's what I want to know.'

'Evans,' said Scannie slowly, 'you are very welcome to join us in the gardens, but unfortunately you'd get your hands dirty, and we know you wouldn't want that, you big wuss!'

Again laughter. Officer Jaipur sidled up to the table. 'Governor wants to see you, Scanlon,' he said meaningfully. There was always a heavy implication in everything he said to the inmates. That was one reason why they didn't like him. One reason.

Scannie rested his elbows on the table. 'I'll see him when I'm ready.'

'You can see him now.'

'Is that what he said, Jaipur?'

Jaipur paused, 'No.'

Evans had more to say, as usual. 'Anything else, Jaipur?'

'Mr Jaipur.'

'All right,' said Scannie. 'I wanna have a chat with him anyway.' He got up, but instead of immediately following Jaipur, Prisoner Scanlon turned and leant over Wilson till his sleeve almost touched his empty plate. He laid a forefinger on the table.

'I want Puzzle with me tomorrow,' he said, 'so I won't be happy if anything should inconvenience that arrangement. Got it?'

When he got there, he found the governor sitting in his high-backed chair talking to someone that Scannie assumed to be a visitor. It was a tall man with long hair and an unshaven face: the sort of person Scannie would have looked down his nose at before all the trouble started.

'Now, Mr Scanlon,' began the governor. 'Have you ever heard of… what is it?'

The visitor spoke in a thin, raspy voice, '*Orchis alterdaphnia*'.

Orchids weren't just an area of expertise for Scannie, they were an obsession. He would spend every waking hour he had to himself reading obscure library books on the flowers, their origin, their culture, and their geography. Though there are thought to be over 30,000 natural varieties and over 120,000 man-made hybrids, he reckoned he could pretty well identify or describe any you might care to throw at him.

'I have,' he said. 'It's a Norfolk monopodial, Or it was. It's been extinct since the mid-nineteenth century.'

The governor polished his glasses, replaced them, and linked his hands behind his chair. He gave a broad smile. 'Now there's a thing,' he said.

*****

Kew Gardens are about ten miles from Pentonville. Scannie was being taken there by prison van to identify an orchid, which he believed would turn out to be a very ordinary orchid and not the extinct variety that this so-called expert claimed. He wasn't in the best of moods. At least Puzzle wouldn't be mucking around on the allotment after having given Jaipur a very generalised opinion of his supposed country of origin and, indeed, parenthood.

Scannie Scanlon was getting old. The other prisoners still respected him more than they respected anyone else, including the screws, but no longer was he the hard man. He couldn't sort someone out like in the old days, back when he had earned his stripes. But he would be the first to admit that he was no angel.

Tobacco smuggling had been a lucrative sideline for him. He could lift up his heel, making his shoe flip out, and pop in a load of good Ready Rubbed. He could do it quick as a flash, so they could never catch him (till they did!). But it's different now: too many drugs and it isn't a game. The best thing that can be done for someone in prison is give them back their self-respect, but no one can respect themselves when they're doing drugs.

Only an idiot would want to work in that sort of climate, but it seems there are plenty of idiots, like Jaipur. Straight out of college, they can quote from their textbooks but have no idea about how to deal with human beings. That's why Scannie was so worried about Martin Puzzle.

Martin wasn't doing well, so it was easy to wind him up. Many of the inmates knew this and took the opportunity to do just that. Scannie realised they would do it all the more when he was away. He thought about bending the governor's ear about Jaipur's unhelpful behaviour, but what was the point? You end up losing Jaipur and getting another idiot in his place because that's all you get these days. Looking back at the years of camaraderie with the old guard, Scanlon had felt sad when each had retired or moved on. It was sadder still these days when he saw who had replaced them.

'Are you all right, Scannie? You've been very quiet,' the driver said.

'S'all right, John. I was somewhere else, that's all.'

'I'm stopping here. There's an escort for you. This orchid you're seeing is kept in a very special place. The likes of us ain't allowed inside, apparently.'

The van stopped, and he was led to a private car by the man he had seen in the governor's office.

'I've never been to Kew Gardens before,' said Scannie, by way of making conversation.

'Nor will you today,' replied the man. 'But we're trusting you not to tell them that.'

'Where are we going then?'

'Wakehurst. S'bout fifty miles. S'at all right?'

'S'pose it'll 'ave to be.'

He knew Wakehurst from the magazines. Wakehurst was a kind of Noah's Ark for seeds of as many plant species as were likely to survive a nuclear holocaust.

'I hear you're trying to grow *orchis dextiphilliac*,' said the man. 'You never will, you know, not in this country, not without controlled conditions.'

Scannie grinned at him. 'We'll have a little bet, shall we? You give me nine months, and I'll show you flowers.'

'I don't bet, but I'll take you on in spirit. I'd like to see what you do.'

'So what about this *alterdaphnia* you think you've got? I'm willing to bet you haven't.'

'We pretty nearly haven't. That's where you come in. But we're going to trust you with a few more secrets before that.'

'Go on then.' Scannie was intrigued.

'You have to sign something first.'

When they arrived at Wakehurst, he had to sign the Official Secrets Act; something he did with a smile on his face (as if he were in a position to spill the beans on any great orchid conspiracy in Pentonville Prison!).

The Millennium Seed Bank consists of three rows of storage units. Each one hosts a unique environment suited to the type of seed being stored. There are plans to build more complex structures as conservationists become increasingly desperate in their efforts to redress the impact of ecological damage. Despite this, there are some seeds that cannot yet be stored, at least as far as anyone knows. Work on such reprobates is undertaken in a secret storage facility underneath the glasshouses, where masks and gowns must be worn to avoid contamination.

'Right,' said the man, 'this is Amelia, and I'm Roger. You have to wear this gown to go in.'

Amelia was the young pretty woman who had walked with them from the car to the reception desk where he had signed the form. She handed him a white gown.

'And there's a mask for when we get down there.'

'Nothing you see or hear,' said Roger, 'goes out of this place.'

'All right,' he replied. 'I'm guessing you two are in the orchid department then.'

'First guess wrong,' he said. 'We're from MI5.'

Stopping in front of a silver door, Amelia said, 'This is the only plant that we keep in here. It's been at Wakehurst since 2009. We put it in the parterre outside at first, but it's started to die, so we've brought it inside where we can keep it in very controlled conditions.'

'What about growing another one from seed?' asked Scannie.

'We've tried and tried and tried. It just won't happen. Now, what do you think?'

She opened the door to reveal an orchid, safely tucked behind a plate glass window, bearing a single flower. Scannie held his breath, and the agents held theirs while he looked.

'I've never seen another one like it,' he said. 'I'll grant you that. But how did you come across such a thing when it's supposed to have been extinct for so long?'

'Woolpit in Suffolk, 1853,' said Roger. 'A woman, we think her name was Laura, predicted the outbreak of war. And she was right, too.'

'Crimean,' said Amelia.

'But as she also predicted the exact date it would end, 26th March 1856, she became a minor celebrity.'

Scannie scratched his head. 'All well and good,' he said, 'but what's that got to do with the orchid?'

'It was her orchid,' said Amelia. 'When it flowers, there is peace in this country, but when the flowers die off, there is war.'

'She had "green" fingers, as they say,' said Roger.

Amelia looked closely at Scannie to discern his level of understanding. 'We don't know where it came from,' she said, 'but some say her ancestors may have been green all over.'

'The authorities took a lot more interest when the Boer War took place,' said Roger. 'It was acquired by the government and kept under close observation.'

'Not everyone was convinced at the time,' said Amelia. 'But those who weren't had to admit that it was a massive coincidence. Then the First World War happened, and that pretty much did it.'

Scannie folded his arms. 'And you're telling me that this orchid predicted the date?'

They nodded gravely.

'And the Armistice? And the Second World War?'

'Yep,' said Roger. 'Throw in the Korean War and the Suez Crisis and you can see what we've got. Mr Scanlon, your reputation goes before you, and so we would like you to examine it and tell us if there is anything we can do.'

'Show me the seeds first,' he said.

The seeds were housed in another part of the vault. There was a good supply. That they had all come from one plant seemed surprising, but he had heard of orchids that lived for over a hundred years, giving them plenty of opportunity to produce seeds. As he expected, they were fairly ordinary: dark in colour, oval in shape, and slightly rough to the touch. They watched closely as he put one to his lips. It made him sneeze.

'Careful!' said Roger.

'Sorry,' he said, twisting his foot around. 'No harm done. Get the orchid then. I'll have a butcher's for you.'

They hurried to the silver door, and he straightened his shoe.

Amelia lifted it out on its stand.

'It's a lovely plant,' said Scannie as he examined it. 'But it is dying. You can see the leaves have all dropped off down this side. In my opinion, it should be outside. All this artificial heating and automatic watering is very clever, but it needs real sunlight.'

'Will that save it? Maybe there's something we could put in the soil?' asked Roger.

'I grow most of them outside.'

'Then let's plant it on your allotment!'

'Roger!' Amelia looked worried.

He tried to reassure her. 'Look, it's going to die here anyway, we all know that. Mr Scanlon is the last chance we have. I think we should take it back with us now.'

Along with a supply of liquefied nutrients, the three of them and the orchid were driven back to Pentonville in the private car. When they arrived, Scannie went to his cell to pick up his little store of gardening equipment.

Martin had not had a good day. He had been involved in several altercations that resulted in him being confined to his cell. Scannie knew how they had started even before he caught the supercilious look on Officer Jaipur's face.

'What are you going to do with those?' asked Jaipur when he saw him walking down the corridor with the tools.

'I know what I'd like to do with them,' he replied, 'but that would make a right mess of your trousers.'

Jaipur sneered at him.

'Course,' he added, 'I wouldn't mind betting you'd enjoy that.'

'All right, Scannie,' said another officer, 'don't start.'

'Where's he supposed to be going?' Jaipur asked.

'He's planting flowers on the allotments.'

'In which case, I insist on accompanying the prisoner.'

There was no doubt that Jaipur had something up his sleeve as he left the main building in the company of Scannie, Roger, and Amelia, but whatever it was never got the chance to be revealed.

There was some sort of accident on the path to the greenhouse. Officer Jaipur had been walking in close proximity to Mr Scanlon: Amelia and Roger were very clear about that, and it was clearly noted in his dismissal proceedings. Then somebody tripped, and the plant was dashed hard onto the ground. Despite the best efforts of Mr Scanlon, the stem was entirely broken and all vitality was completely irretrievable. After Roger had helped the weeping Amelia away from the little allotment strips, Scannie never saw anyone from MI5 again, and he was left alone in the greenhouse pondering the events of the day.

Soon he would be back in the prison eating dinner with everyone except Martin, who was still "resting". Scanlon switched on his little radio and caught the news. There was trouble in the South China Sea: American warships were moving closer to Taiwan, and Britain, as America's closest ally, would be expected to support them. Whatever trouble there was to come, it would be over in nine months. Scannie flipped off his shoe and poured some seeds into his hand: oval, dark in colour, and slightly rough to the touch. He raised them to his lips and blew warm, wet air from deep in his chest.

Look after your prisoners. Let them tend flowers.

15. THE TAXI DRIVER AND THE BANSHEE

'This turning here.' Ian's thin-lipped passenger, who had insisted on sitting behind him, avoided looking into his mirror as she snapped her directions. He had become a good judge of fares who didn't engage in general conversation, more's the pity, and it didn't take the intuition of a taxi driver to see how stressed she was. He had the gift of that reassuring Barnsley twang that is so often a benediction to the out-of-love, the out-of-work, and the out-of-sorts; and he certainly believed that it had inspired some good tips. She needn't have bothered giving him directions once she had stated the destination because he knew the house: he had grown up there.

'By the pillar box,' he said with a grin as she started to open her mouth. She nodded in assent and fiddled in her fussy little handbag as he slowed down. He thought she must be in her late fifties: that age between believing youthful appearances can be retained without adjustment and the falling away of natural femininity that pre-empts the long crabbed resilience of old age. Her small purse matched the scale of her handbag, but Ian didn't give up.

Indicating the gloomy façade of the detached old building, he said with what might have been taken as irreverence, 'D'you get the odd thing going bump in the night? I mean in the back bedroom there?'

The rustling stopped, and she raised her shoulders. He gave his Barnsley chuckle. 'I used to live there, see, when I was a kid, like, and that was my bedroom.'

Even in the dark, he could see that she had blanched. His attempt at geniality had completely misfired.

'What rubbish!' she snapped, giving him the exact fare and no more.

He left her to it with a curt "ta" and was soon enveloped in the silence of the road. She stood at the gate a few moments, seemingly lost in thought.

*****

Business in that particular suburb of North London wasn't as good as it had been when the company started, but even so Big Jim didn't like to see the lads playing cards while they waited for the phone to ring. The early evening had little to offer after the last commuter train had squirmed past the platform. He had tried sending them out on spec, but if there was a sudden rush, then no one was available to take the jobs. He hunched his shoulders over some paperwork and grumbled. Ian had just won Trumps, and his boyish yelps were beyond annoying. Perhaps there were too many cabbies for his little firm, especially in this recession. He consoled himself with the thought that Ian would be gone soon enough anyway, now that the lad had finished his PhD. When the phone eventually rang, he was disappointed to find it wasn't for a fare.

'Ian,' he deliberately cut through the mirth. 'Are you the fellow who took a certain Mrs Ayles to Havensmere Road last night.'

Ian remembered the fare well. It didn't matter that she hadn't given her name when he picked her up from Higham Hill Station. Ayles. He pondered on the name. He thought of an old school friend: an odd boy, not really a friend at all.

'Yes, I took a fare to Havensmere.'

'Funny,' said Jim, handing him the phone. ''Cause I thought you was a fat git!'

Rolf sniggered, and Ian feigned a kick at him as he took the receiver. 'Hello, luv. What can I do you for?'

He pictured the young Ayles boy he had known at infant school: an unusual character who never showed any emotion. He tried to recall what had become of him as the woman made her request.

'No, sorry luv, I can't do that,' he said. 'I'm working.' Jim raised his eyebrows, and Ian mouthed an obscenity in his direction, but it was obvious that something was amusing him.

'Well, if you pay me for the time, but don't get your hopes up too much.' Rolf instigated a suggestive whoop causing Ian to hold the phone away from his face in an attempt to supress his laughter. Jim waved a warning at the others to be quiet as they barked out their opinions of Ian's luck.

'Right, give me fifteen minutes, and we'll see what we can do.'

Putting the phone down, Ian pushed Rolf off his chair. Rolf, now virtually helpless with a fit of the giggles, obligingly tumbled.

'Hey, hey,' Jim intervened. 'What was all that about? You 'aven't pulled, 'ave you?'

'No, I bloody haven't!' he emphasised. 'She's a horrible old bird. She just wants to know about the ghosts in the house I took her to because I used to live there, that's all.'

'You're not going out telling ghost stories on *my* time!' Jim heavily laid down the law.

'No, I'm not, your Lordship,' he replied as he donned his jacket. 'I'm taking her for a drive up to Hazledene Square at the normal rate, and I'll spin her some yarn on the way... Rolfie! Shut it!'

At the far side of twilight, most of the houses in Havensmere had put on their lights, but not number 31. The only detached building in the street, it stood in complete darkness. Ian guessed that something about its position, historical status, or saleability had spared it from the bulldozer when the new estate had been built. It still bore the name "Havensmere House", implying that it had been central to the original estate. He frowned slightly as he remembered the odd schoolfellow who shared the name of his sponsor and how uneasy he had felt when they were together. He shivered. He hadn't liked him at all.

Mrs Ayles appeared as soon as he pulled up. She hurried to the cab and looked furtively up and down the lonely street as he leaned over and opened the front passenger door for her to embark. It wasn't a particularly cool night, but when she clambered in, he was suddenly aware of the cold, as if she had been standing in chilly night air. He thought of young Ayles. His mother had often used the epithet "strange and unusual" to describe the schoolboy, but that had been a long time ago. He vaguely recalled that the lad had come to a bad end.

'Right you are,' he said warily as he switched on the meter. 'Hazledene Square, yeah?'

Hazledene Square was a couple of miles farther on into the next borough. He took a slow drive down a wooded avenue before turning round and heading back to Havensmere Road. To his chagrin, she asked short questions and left the silences for him to do most of the talking. He found himself having to be voluble on the subject of the supernatural, something he had rejected in all its forms many years ago.

'My old nan said the thing followed us down here,' he told her as she pressed him to recall the incidents there. 'From Barnsley'.

'And your mother?'

'Nah, she doesn't do any of that stuff.' His mother was completely rational, he thought, and a good thing too. Then he made the mistake of telling her that he had suffered from what were called "night terrors" as a child. She instantly latched onto it.

'I'm not a psychiatrist,' he said. 'You know it probably had nothing to do with the house, or ghosts, or anything, but it wasn't very nice, whatever it was.'

He grimaced to himself, wishing he hadn't agreed to meet her. The nosy woman wanted to know everything about his illness. And that's all it was: everyone gets ill. He could still remember having shaking fits and doors jamming shut, but he also remembered the chocolate his rational mother used to give him. Mrs Ayles had no interest in chocolate.

'Funny,' he persisted, 'I've got a physics degree, you know. I'd mostly say ghosts were rubbish myself, but... I dunno... all those bangs and crashes... Perhaps it was draughts. Up north, we aren't supposed to mind a bit of a breeze in our houses, are we?' He was going to add, 'unlike you soft Southerners,' but they had reached the house and he wasn't enjoying the reminiscence.

The rational world was much easier to deal with: Euler equations that explain why smoke from a dying bonfire took on a corporeal aspect in low wind or molecular models that demonstrate why different woods creak with contrasting voices when the temperature changes. So when she invited him in to continue their conversation, he declined with a convenient excuse.

'Sorry, luv, I'd 'ave to keep the meter running,'

'Keep it running then,' she was quite serious.

He shuffled awkwardly.

'Well, we're not supposed to do that,' he replied. She took a £50 note out of her bag. 'Aw no,' he objected. 'Come on, luv. We don't have to play games.'

'This is no game. I need to know more.'

Pocketing the note, he followed her helplessly. 'I've just done me PhD. I don't know what everyone's gonna think. I'm supposed to be the scientist, me.'

The inside of the house was a dirty, smelly mess of curled mats and stained chairs. Mouldy wallpaper peeled away at the edges and he nearly tripped where the batten had come away from the carpet. When she opened the kitchen door, he gagged at the smell of dead animal. It had a broken hinge and no inside handle, so it could only be opened with the large key hanging from a key ring at an angle to the lock. She took the key out of the lock and hung it on a bracket. He stared down the hall while she fiddled with an ancient kettle.

'It were upstairs mainly, all the noises and that,' he continued.

'But didn't your mother hear the noises?'

'I suppose.' He sat down carefully.

'I'd like to meet your mother.'

'She's in Barnsley.'

'When she next comes to see you then.'

He stared grimly down the corridor. 'Yeah, maybe.' Of course, she wouldn't be allowed anywhere near his mother. 'I don't want anything to drink by the way,' he said as she started to make the brew. She ignored him.

BANG!

He leapt up. 'Oh hell!'

He looked around. The maddening sound had come from above. The back bedroom maybe?

'That's it, I'm off, time's up.' The light tone he adopted was an attempt to disguise a tremendous wave of nausea that he hadn't felt for many years.

'Not yet,' she snapped, opening a drawer.

'Sorry, luv, someone will come later with yer change from the fifty quid.' And he was absolutely determined that it wouldn't be him.

He stood up, but she had already stepped ahead of him and unhooked the key. He tutted and headed to the door, which suddenly closed by itself.

'Aw, come on!' His exaggerated Barnsley accent was forced because now he could clearly remember those half-forgotten terrors. He had the feel of them, the taste of them, and the reason for them. He spun round, gracelessly took the key from her, and gave her a push towards the open drawer. Turning the key in the lock, he felt it move slowly as though it were in covered in thick treacle.

As he glanced back, he saw her, eyes blazing, holding a knife by its blade. Her open mouth looked like the surprised expression on a painted doll. He yelled, and she flung it at him. It stuck fast in the bone above his knee. Howling hopelessly, he stumbled around the room, crashing into shelves and chairs. In a flash, she had another knife in her hand. He opened the kitchen door and grabbed the outer handle to pull it shut on her. The door was stiff. As it closed, the blade of the knife cracked through the thin wood just above the handle, nicking his hand. He held the door closed while his free hand gripped the knife in his leg. It took a herculean effort to pull out the blade.

Letting go of the door handle, he hopped agonisingly to the front door. Just as he got there, she opened the kitchen door and flung another knife at him. The blade stuck in his calf. He pulled at it, yelling as hard as he could. So much for physics. So much for Euler. So much for murder! Trying to wrench the door ajar was like fighting through a gelatinous portal from one of his childhood nightmares, but wrench it open he did, the blood bubbling under his dark trousers. He tumbled through screaming.

He crawled to the car on his hands and knees. The steering column became red and gruesome with dark blood. He started the engine and hurled the car around without putting on his seatbelt.

There was no traffic along the dark road, but in his delirious weakness he took the T-junction too fast, putting himself in the path of a white van. His training and remaining presence of mind got him across with merely a clip to the back end of the car, but disorientation and the extra speed caused him to strike a lamp-post with enough force to send him through the windscreen. In his final few moments of screeching sensibility, he heard the car's alarm go off.

*****

Ian came to in hospital. It was fortunate that the man in the white van had been a medic in the Marines otherwise the knife wounds alone would have caused him to bleed to death. But he didn't know any of that. All he knew was that his leg was strapped up in front of him, and there was a pain somewhere in his head.

And there was Rolf.

'You've lost your job, mate,' he said helpfully.

Ian looked away. Even before he'd seen him, Ian had wanted to scream. He did so, and it worked wonders.

'I'm afraid Mr Dunsford can't have visitors just yet,' said one of the three nurses who quickly surrounded his bed.

*****

He was sent home after only two nights. Bandaged and bruised, Ian went upstairs, wrapped a towel around his throbbing forehead, and sat on the side of the bath. He noticed he was still trembling. He was scared. He had lost his job, the police were hassling him, and he was still in a lot of pain. It couldn't get any worse, he thought.

Suddenly, the bathroom door closed of its own accord. He fell against it sobbing and pulled at the handle till it came off. He was shaking so much he could hardly use his mobile phone, and he spent a long fumbling minute scratching at the screen.

'Rolfie…' he whimpered.

His friend got to him quickly and used a ladder to get in through the bathroom window.

'That door was open all along, mate,' said Rolf. 'All you had to do was pull. It wasn't even on the latch, look.'

'No, no, no,' Ian shook his head. 'It was... it wasn't... Oh God! Oh God!'

*****

Jim paid off the van man in cash, rather more and rather sooner than through the insurance. The bloke was decent enough. He had never liked Havensmere and sympathised with Ian's story.

'I pass the place every day on my rounds,' he said. 'It's always full of druggies'.

Jim was short of a driver. He would rather have lost muddle-headed Rolf than Ian, but the incident had only pre-empted the inevitable. Now that Ian had finished his course, he would be applying for professorships or whatever and would have quit anyway. Jim felt terrible but if the house was, as the police said, uninhabited and there were no signs of knives or persons therein, then it was difficult to prove anything. Losing Ian kept his insurers happy.

It was strange to see him so changed, going on about doors closing and black shapes coming for him. Jim put it down to too much studying.

'Go back up North,' he had said to him. 'See your mother, have a break'.

That seemed to be the sensible option. Ian couldn't stay at Rolf's house forever, nor could he face going home, but he hesitated before phoning. He didn't want to scare her. He didn't want to scare himself.

'What do you mean you were attacked?' she said when he finally got through. 'You can't lose your job if you're attacked. You should get compensation. Why don't you go to a union?' His mother was as predictable as expected.

'I'm not in a union!'

'What's wrong, Ian? Why aren't you at your house?' She rattled on and on, making him increasingly agitated.

'Because... because I'm having some kind of nervous breakdown.'

'But you said you were attacked.'

'Yes, and then it all happened. All this stupid stuff that I don't believe in.' There was silence at the other end. 'Mum?'

'What sort of stuff, Ian?'

He felt stupid telling her. He didn't think his mother had ever taken his childhood stories seriously, but she was listening now.

'Oh, doors opening and jamming shut.'

'Who attacked you?' she asked quietly.

'It was... well, this mad woman.'

'Did she say her name?'

'She called herself Mrs Ayles. I think she...'

'Ian,' she interrupted him with a dry voice, 'can you stay with Rolf till I get there?'

'What is it, Mum?'

*****

Rolf was relieved when, the following day, he went to meet his mother and then book into a B & B. It had been a nightmare coping with Ian in his odd state while his missus and their kid were in the house. Apparently, doors were still opening and closing on their own, and now Ian was hearing things. There is only so much you can do for a mate, especially if you value your marriage. He walked into work with a spring in his step, despite himself.

''Ere,' said Jim, 'don't spread this, but I think that Mrs Ayles called again. It sounded like her. She asked for Ian again.'

'Blimey!'

'So do I tell the coppers or do I keep schtum?'

*****

Mrs Dunsford liked a drink at midday, and St Pancras Station had a large pub on its upper level. Ian ordered a cup of tea that tasted of iron. He looked at her. She was a bulky woman in her early sixties, ready to crack a joke or relate, wide-eyed, the latest scandals from the TV soaps. She took her brandy in funereal sips.

'You're scaring me,' he said.

'I know,' she said. 'I'm scaring me as well.' She drained the glass. 'Do you remember why we moved from Barnsley?'

'All sorts of reasons,' he bluffed, almost knowing what she was going to say.

'Do you remember your night terrors? Well, they were the reason we moved, but it didn't make any difference.' He creased his forehead. 'You see, Ian, we have a banshee in our family, and it's all my fault.'

'What's a banshee when it's at home?' He would have laughed at her if she had told him this at any other time, but he wasn't laughing now.

'It's a vengeful spirit.'

He leant on his elbows and regarded her as though searching for any inconsistency he could find to make this whole thing stop.

She went on, 'It's taking its revenge on you because of something I did.'

'What did you do?' he asked slowly.

'Remember when you were little? You had a friend called Malcolm; he went to your infant school. You were good friends at first. Then, you see, you stopped playing with him. He was a funny little boy. He was always rubbing his tummy. I don't know why. I shouldn't wonder if nowadays they would say he had learning difficulties. The thing is, you used to always go out when he came round.'

'Malcolm Ayles,' said Ian. 'Didn't he fall out of a tree or something? We had a memorial service for him.' His mother looked him straight in the face.

'He was an odd boy,' she went on. 'Strange and unusual. Even though you weren't there, he insisted on coming into the house. He'd stand there talking to me with his serious face for ages and ages. Then he'd start to do the washing-up. I should have sent him home, but he was so lonely, poor little boy. So strange and most unusual.'

'But we weren't really friends,' Ian tried to justify himself, 'and he never played with me at school. In fact, he never played any games at all. He just sat on the benches and watched us. He wasn't right. Some teacher should have taken notice or something. You said it yourself, he was strange and unusual.'

'He couldn't reach the sink,' said Mrs Dunsford, 'to do the washing-up, so one day I piled up some boxes for him, but he fell.' She was silent.

'He fell out of a tree.'

'No. He was found under a tree. I took him to the woods when you were all asleep.'

'You carried his dead body to the woods and left him there?' He stared at her.

'I didn't kill him, Ian!'

'Why couldn't you have…?'

'Why d'you think?'

Ian couldn't think. He opened his mouth, closed it, and opened it again. 'And now he's come back, you say?'

She spoke quietly and deliberately. 'No, Ian. It's his mother, Betty Ayles. She went into a home. The last thing I heard was that she'd died of broken heart. Because of Malcolm... because of us.'

Ian stood up. 'Oh no! Hang on... this woman was real. She threw knives! She even paid me fifty quid, *and* they all heard her on the telephone! No, mum, this Mrs Ayles was no bloody banshee or whatever!'

*****

Later that day, a fare took Rolf conveniently close to Havensmere. His curiosity getting the better of him, he decided to stop there and have a look around. He went back to the taxi and called Jim.

'You won't believe this,' he said, 'I'm at Havensmere. I've found Ian's woman.'

'God, Rolfie! What are you doing to me? How do you know it's her?'

'It's her, I'm sure of it. I hid behind the fence and videoed her on my phone. She was picking flowers and going on about spirits taking over dead people. That's a clue, isn't it? You just listen to this lark!' He put his phone close to the taxi radio and turned the volume up. Jim could just make out the mad ravings.

'O spirit, spirit, soon you will be returned to life. You will take back the life that was stolen from you... O hemlock... O mandrake poison...'

'See?' Rolf snapped his phone shut. 'It must be her.'

'I'll phone the police,' said Jim. 'You get back here. Now!'

'I'll be right with you.'

Jim phoned the coppers and reported Mrs Ayles last call as he repeated Rolf's story. They were more interested than he expected.

'Call in all your drivers, and don't answer the door till we get there,' they told him, 'and warn Mr Dunsford as soon as you get hold of him.'

But Rolf was still curious. He sneaked back to the end of the fence, but she was gone. He slipped through the gate and walked up to the boarded window. She came round the side of the house and up behind him, chanting.

'He is come to us, he is...' Rolf turned and faced her as her hideous visage went from ecstasy to fury. She screamed and dropped the flowers. He backed up against the wall.

'You fool!' she snarled and thrust the pointed blade of a knife through his Adam's apple.

*****

St Pancras to Higham Hill Station takes a little more than half an hour; long enough for Ian to ponder the awful prospect of returning to Havensmere House. He had tried to reason with his mother, tried to persuade her to tell the police, but now even he no longer kept faith with the rational. If they were to be free of it, she assured him, they would have to face the spirit that she insisted was Mrs Ayles in Havensmere House together.

*****

Rolf tried to get the knife out, but the strength left his arms each time he raised them up. He couldn't taste the blood that he saw rolling down his chest because of the overwhelming pain in the back of his tongue. Its glistening ruby wreath startled him. Shock made his twisting, shaking legs feel distant and unreal as he tumbled to the floor. His eyes bulged, and the back of his hands struck the ground repeatedly as a white van pulled up to the house.

*****

The first thing the young policeman did when he got to the taxi office was to ask Jim where Ian was.

'He's gone up town to meet his mum. That's what Rolf reckons. What about this Mrs Ayles? What's she all about exactly?'

The young policeman puffed himself up as he answered, 'She's absconded from somewhere or other, somewhere she was being kept for her own good.' He would have said more, but his radio crackled into life. 'Oh no!' he said when he heard the message. 'I'll be there right away.'

Jim tailed him to the door, 'What is it? Is it Ian?'

'No, it's your other driver, Rolf.'

*****

By the time the paramedics reached Havensmere House, the van driver had already performed a tracheotomy and was carrying out a chest compression. Rolf had lost a lot of blood, but the man had managed to keep a sideways pressure on the knife so that it almost closed the yawning hole in his vein. The paramedics kept the knife pushed down as they eased him onto the stretcher. As they loaded him into the ambulance, the policeman arrived. By late afternoon, the place had been cordoned off, and forensics had taken what they needed.

*****

The cordon of orange tape and warning signs was easily negotiated by Mrs Dunsford and her son. Although the door had been secured, Ian noticed that one of the plywood boards on the window had come away.

'Look there,' he said, 'that's blood. It's still red. This cordon isn't for what happened to me.'

His mother pulled at the bent plywood by way of answer, and it crashed down across the concrete patio. There was no glass in the window, so she stepped over the sill and looked in.

'Mrs Ayles, Mrs Ayles,' she whispered. 'I am sorry. I am so sorry. Please don't hurt my son. He did nothing. It was all me.' She climbed in.

'Mum,' Ian breathed loudly. It was silent in the dim decrepit room. He peered warily behind him and then followed her into the darkness of a short hallway. 'Mum,' he whispered more urgently.

She looked up at the collapsed stairs. 'Can you feel how cold it is?' she asked. 'It shouldn't be this cold.'

'She's not here,' said Ian. 'Let's go.'

His mother turned back and looked into the kitchen. He stifled a choking feeling.

'Empty,' she said despairingly.

'Let's go,' said Ian, wearing his bravado as an alpine skier might wear a grass skirt. The door they had used to get into the hallway was half open. He pulled it towards him. Suddenly, the silhouette of Mrs Ayles appeared before him. He shrieked and stumbled back against the wall.

'No!' cried Mrs Dunsford, thrusting herself between them.

'He's here!' wailed Mrs Ayles. 'He's here!'

Ian screamed and covered his face as a thick blackness swayed in their mist. She threw something. Ian clutched his chest and fell to the floor shaking.

'Forgive me!' Mrs Dunsford shouted, but the black thing grew until it seemed to envelop them all. The two women embraced in its gloom and then fell to the floor. As quickly as it grown, the darkness subsided.

Ian was certain he had felt the knife penetrate his chest, but when he opened his jacket and put a tentative hand inside his shirt, he found it had barely nicked his skin. The knife lay on the floor. He stood up and, rubbing his tummy, stepped over the two dead women. A full moon shone through the gap where the plywood board had been removed. He clambered through and walked onto the calm street. It was an odd world, he thought, strange and unusual; strange and unusual.

16. THE SAUSAGES THAT SOLVE ALL YOUR PROBLEMS

'Mind the stepladder, love,' called Teresa as Rachel, looking frazzled after her long journey, burst in through the front door. She turned off the gas on the hob to stop the sausages in the pan from sizzling as her daughter dragged box after box out of the taxi and into the cottage.

'Down, Bertie! Down!' shouted Rachel as their labrador leapt up at her, barking and panting. 'Mum, you'll never believe it… Ian, my line-manager, won't give me the report till Friday 'cos it's got to be data-checked. The minister wants it on his desk first thing tomorrow as well as the final version of the commissioner's agenda. I don't know what they think…'

'Have a sausage,' interrupted her mother.

The young woman looked at her and opened her mouth.

'Go on,' repeated Teresa. 'It's just the one. Then you can tell me the problem again.'

'I'm not eating sausages! I've just got in. I've been five hours on a train and nearly another hour getting across Exeter in a rotten taxi! Let me get in first, can't you? And can't you get this stepladder out of the way? That's twice I've nearly tripped over it. Get down, Bertie!'

Teresa forked a sausage out of the pan and held it high in the air. 'It's important.'

'It's not important! It's a sausage! Anyway, I thought you'd turned vegetarian.'

'I've turned back for today.'

'Why?'

'Because these are special sausages. I bought them off a gypsy in Moretonhampstead.'

The taxi revved its engine impatiently.

'Right,' Rachel turned round dismissively. 'I'm going to get the rest of my stuff.'

On leaving Oxford, Rachel had taken a job as an advisor to a Foreign Office minister, which involved travelling abroad for large parts of the year. This made it impossible for her to put down permanent roots, so she periodically came back to her mother's cottage on Dartmoor. After two further journeys with her arms filled with boxes, she had piled all her belongings in the hall.

'You'll never get all that in your little room,' said Teresa. 'Not with the new bed.'

'You knew I was going to bring my things back. Why is all your art stuff here? It's taking up all the room!'

'It's my house!'

Rachel put down the last of the boxes and sighed. Teresa proffered the sausage again, and Bertie resumed his barking.

'You eat this while I feed Bertie. He's such a stupid dog. I had to take him to the vet last week. Next door's cat lures him to the apple tree, climbs onto the lower branches, and then scratches him to bits.'

'He never learns, does he?'

'No, and that vet is getting quite expensive.'

Rachel took the fork and bit into the sausage. She chewed thoughtfully and then said, 'Mum! Why can't your art stuff go under the stairs for now? Look.' She pushed open the door to the stair cupboard with her foot. 'See? There's loads of space! And all my stuff can go in the basement. The whole place will be so much tidier.' She popped more of the sausage into her mouth.

'I told you these were special sausages.' Teresa opened a can of dog food and Bertie panted his appreciation. 'They solve all your problems. That's what the gypsy said.'

'How ridiculous!'

'It's not. We had a problem at work the other day with the fishing restrictions off the Kent coast. They said if we didn't impose them, we would lose all the Dover sole, but if we did, then that would put the fisherman out of work... So, I had a sausage.'

'You had a sausage?'

'Yes, and then it occurred to me. Crabs.'

'Crabs?'

'Yes, there are no restrictions on crabs. There's a big demand for them in France, so they can all fish for crabs instead. Problem solved. And it's all because of the sausages.'

'I don't believe that. How can sausages do that?'

'I don't know,' admitted Teresa as she forked tinned meat into the dog's dish. 'And I don't think the gypsy did either. But they certainly work. What about your problem? What will you do about getting the data to the minister?'

Rachel sat down and nibbled more of the sausage. Suddenly, she rose up out of her seat. 'I have it!' she cried. 'Of course! I'll give Ian the agenda, and he can sort it himself! Then it's his neck on the line if it's not in on time. I'll call the minister now. Brilliant!'

'You see,' said her mother, 'they do work!'

'Then you'd better get some more.'

'I can't. That gypsy said they were the only ones of their kind.'

'Did she now.'

A loud knocking at the door broke their mutual silence.

'Oh, that'll be Peter from the other side of the square,' said Teresa. 'He's back from university, and I've been helping him with his assignments.'

Their fourteenth-century cottage was part of a small hamlet in one of the loneliest corners of Dartmoor. Theirs and the other dozen or so dwellings were arranged in a higgledy-piggledy approximation of a square. About half were second homes and unoccupied most of the time. The rest secreted aging playboys, artists, disgraced film directors, and the like from the general glare of society, making it a hamlet much like any other in those parts.

'Hello Peter,' she said. 'Would you mind carrying the stepladder outside for me?'

The lanky youth, son of a South African arms trader, opened the back door. In an instant, Bertie the dog was out of his basket woofing manically through the glass at next door's cat, which had miraculously materialised. It hissed back wildly.

'I'll tell you what, maybe you could do it later.' Teresa took Bertie by his collar and led him away from the door. 'Calm down, Bertie! Calm down!'

Peter shut the door. 'I'm already having trouble, and it's not even the Part Ones yet!' he said. 'I'm never going to get through at this rate.'

'Show me how far you've got.'

'I haven't got anywhere. It's to do with to do with using x to the power of $n-1$ to work out heat dynamics in the core of the sun. I tell you, I literally have no idea. But if I do it as a straight calculus exercise, it'll take me ages.'

Rachel turned her head to the window through which she could see the cat sitting in the apple tree staring down at the duck pond.

'Have a sausage,' said Teresa.

Peter frowned. 'A what?'

'A sausage. Here, I'll give you a knife and fork.'

The student carefully sliced it up and ate it bit by tiny bit. As he raised the last morsel to his lips, he froze. Teresa and Rachel watched bemused.

'It's a bell curve!' he whispered. They looked at each other. 'Don't you see? The centre isn't the hottest part, so it has to be... yes! It's a Gaussian distribution!'

In a trice, he was up and demanding a pencil and paper. While the search for such things was underway, he capered around the kitchen on the tip of his toes. Once kitted out with the requisite stationery, he hurled himself out of the cottage singing "Gaussian distribution" to the tune of "The Skye Boat Song".

'Amazing,' said Rachel, after he had left. 'I'm sort of coming round to agreeing with you about those sausages.'

Teresa switched on the radio and they just caught the end of the news, which mentioned more fighting in the Middle East. 'I've had enough of hearing about that today,' she said and switched it off again. 'I can't understand why we're still trading with some of these regimes.'

'If we do, we're seen as sanctioning their human rights abuses, and if we don't, their economies fail, their people starve, and there's more support for extremism. It's an insoluble problem.'

Her mother gave her a strange look. 'Or is it?' she asked.

Rachel turned her head slowly. 'Sausages?' she mouthed.

'I've got eight left,' said Teresa softly. 'Mightn't that be enough to bring peace for years to come?'

Rachel looked through the back door at the mystery of Dartmoor stretching into the distance: its blue tors visible above and around the old apple tree, whose long low branches reflected smoothly in the duck pond. 'Save them,' she said, 'for the sake of our children's children.'

*****

The following day, Rachel got an urgent call and had to return to London. The latest flare-up in the Middle East was sending diplomatic shock waves through the West, and, as usual, Whitehall was expected to square the circle. A car picked her up at 6am, and she didn't expect to return till the end of the week.

Teresa didn't have to be back at work for several more days, so she thought she would take the opportunity to have a good tidy. But before she could get started, Peter turned up with his Matrix Gaussian Distribution. She perused it closely.

'Well done,' she said. 'They'll be impressed with that. If anything, you've probably gone into too much detail. All you have to do now is draw the curve.'

'Thanks to you,' he replied. 'And thanks to the sausages. Oh! Look at Bertie! That cat's teasing him again!'

Bertie had his nose pressed against the bottom window of the back door and was barking ferociously at the cat, which was safe behind the glass.

'Come on Bertie,' said Teresa. 'Time for your walk.'

*****

Rachel phoned a couple of days later.

'You'll never guess what I've been up to,' said Teresa. 'I've just finished my painting of our old apple tree. It's mostly oil, but I used gouache for the duck pond to get the reflections.' She paused. 'Another sausage, as if you didn't guess.'

'Mum! Don't eat any more! Do you remember what we talked about the night before I left?'

'Bertie?'

'No! The Middle East problem! The Foreign Secretary is in Torquay tomorrow for a conference. Ian suggested I should invite him over to ours for dinner. We could give him one of the sausages while we talk about the flare-up. Just imagine, he could sort out the whole Lebanon issue and everything!'

'For the sake of our children and our children's children.'

'I've already invited him. He'll be there tomorrow at five. I'll try to get back earlier. Sorry, Mum, got to run.'

Teresa swept, dusted, and tidied everything and everywhere. Her painting of the apple tree, wet though it was, took pride of place in the hall. Rachel arrived at 3:30 p.m. She changed, checked her evening dress in the mirror so carefully that there was not so much as half a fold out of place, and combed her long dark hair seven times. An hour later, the bell rang. He was early.

The two women dashed downstairs. Teresa opened the door and performed something so gracious that it might have been both a bow and a curtsy in front of the surprised minister. She then moved modestly off to the kitchen. The minister's quaint apologies for his early arrival trailed behind her as Rachel led him into the living room for an aperitif.

'Ooh... umm, er...' he mumbled appreciatively as he sat thoughtfully in the least dog-savaged of the chairs.

'As you can see,' explained Rachel, 'we like to keep things simple here in the middle of Dartmoor.'

'Ooh... ah, yes.'

'Is your sherry all right?'

'Ooh... ah, yes.'

'It should be room temperature, but it may have been a bit too near the window.'

'Ooh... umm, right.'

'Do you like sausages?'

'Ooh... ah, well...'

'I don't know how this latest development in the Middle East is going to pan out, but I expect you have some thoughts on that matter yourself, don't you, Minister?'

'Ooh... ah, well... um, yes.'

'Would you excuse me one moment,' she said.

Walking to the doorway, she leaned out of the living room to signal to her mother waiting in the kitchen, who frantically signalled back. The Foreign Secretary tried to see what was going on, but the girl had carefully blocked his view.

It was only when Teresa, frying-pan in hand, turned to face the stove that she saw the carnage. The greasy remains of half-eaten sausages and soggy packaging were spread liberally across the grey flagstones, now starred with doggy footprints.

'BERTIE!' she howled hopelessly.

Looking through the glass door, she saw the stepladder resting against the side of the apple tree where the labrador had dragged it and stood it upright. Bertie himself was halfway up, his hind legs on the middle rung. His forepaws were pushing on one of the low branches, causing it to rise and fall rhythmically while he barked victoriously. At the far end of the branch was the bedraggled cat, clinging tightly despite being dipped in and out of the duck pond.

17. THE GOBLIN OF GOFF'S CORNER

'If you ask about the goblin, they won't tell you. Not the folk round here, not the people of Metfield anyway. Nasty little things, goblins. I don't know why anyone would want to bother.'

Kraark!

(Shut up, Goblin! You revel in it. You love to be told you're nasty.)

Nasty! Faagh!

'So I think we should take the road down to Fressingfield and ask there. We could even try at The Fox and Goose. If we don't manage to find any goblinlore there, at least we'll get a drink.'

Burp!

(Not you! You're bad enough without any drink.)

'We could walk down there, but as we're just popping in for a bit of research, I suggest we drive.'

*****

'Right, let's have a pint now we're here. Cheers!

'Yes, you're right. It does look bigger on the inside than you'd expect from the outside. That's true of a lot of country pubs. You're from the city, aren't you? Is that where you do all your writing? ...Well, there's nothing much to speak of in Metfield. There used to be an old inn, but that was turned into a tea shop years ago. Looks like a few of the locals are in. That's Mick Stern over there, but I

wouldn't talk to him yet. That bloke with him is Toady
Mull, see? Over there, in the raincoat? You want to steer
clear of Toady, mind. He's not local. Lives opposite Richard
Alcott's workshop, where Mick works, just over the other
side of that little brook we passed on the way here. I'll point
it out on the way back. Well, I suppose we could try The
Swan. I'll finish this first. Hello, it looks like those two are
off again!'

'...What do you want, Toady? You're not going to start
on about Brexit again, are you?'

'I know what you think, Mick, and that's your opinion.
It's a done deal now anyway.'

'So, what do you want?'

'A favour. Information.' .

'Why should I do you any favours?'

'What does Alcott do with his cleaning stuff?'

'Disposes of it responsibly.'

'Liar!'

'Leave it out, Toady!'

'He chucks it in the brook, I know that for a fact.'

'No, you don't!'

'I'll find out anyway.'

'You leave me out of this.'

'I can't. You work for him, you're implicated. Damaging
the environment and all that.

'What do you care about the environment...'

'I'll tell you what, let's leave them to it and wander over
to The Swan. There'll be some locals there you could talk
to. Try asking the barmaid. Her family have lived there for
generations. If there's a goblin, they'll know about it. All
right then, but I wouldn't mind another beer. Look, they're
still at it!'

'...That so-called workshop has been built on a floodplain, it should never have been allowed. I've got the parish council on my side.'

'Get lost, Toady, before I hit you.'

'You'll be hearing from my lawyers before long. You all will...'

'Toady's got a property he wants to develop, but he can't because it's next to Alcott's, where Mick works. Oh hi, Mick.'

'Wotcha. Who's your mate?'

'He's up from London. He's a researcher, a folklorist, he calls himself. Want a drink?'

'No, I'm all right, mate. I'm just gonna have this one, then I'm back to work.'

'Mick's a joiner. He works for Richard Alcott. They make high spec cabinets and fancy tables, mostly for Londoners, I wouldn't mind betting.'

'Yeah, when anyone wants them, we do. The trade's getting thin these days because of all the machinery... Toady? Well, he is what he is. No one likes him. I don't know why he bothers coming in here.'

'Usually pops in when he wants something, eh Mick?'

'That's about the measure of him... Goblins? Round here? I dunno. D'you mean the one in the Citroën? Well, I can't stand around all day talking about goblins, I've got work to do'.

Brumm! Brumm! My car!

(Not your car!)

'Some people say they've seen the goblin in a Citroën Dyane. Years ago, there was one that overturned in a ditch near here. Anyway, according to my watch we've got time to quickly nip over to The Swan... Well yes, we could try it this evening instead. I say "we" because you'll need someone with you to break the ice... Me? Of course, always pleased to be of service. Now, I wouldn't mind a half of

that dark one to finish... Fair enough then, we'll head
straight back to Metfield if you want.'

*****

Stop! Stop! Stop!

'If you stop here, you'll see where it's all supposed to
have started. Just by this S-bend coming up. Apparently, the
overturned car broke something open and set him free.
There's nothing to see now though.

'Be careful, it's going to be muddy. I think I'm all right,
but I'm not going over that ditch. Just over there, they
found a load of mediaeval crockery and a strange sort of
hook.'

My hook! My hook!

(Yes, all right, your hook.)

'Some people think it's the goblin's hook... For
grabbing things that aren't his.'

All mine!

'They take things that don't belong to them. Horrible
nasty things!'

Kraark!

(That's a compliment, Goblin!)

'How do they get about? All sorts of ways. They can
vanish and reappear, they can run quite fast, and they can
fly when they want to.'

Heehee! Me! Whee!

(Stop that! You're making me dizzy!)

'They're sort of related to fairies.'

WHAT!

(Sort of, I said.)

'This one came over from France with a priest called
Walkelin.'

L'habit ne fait pas le moine.

(Shut up, Goblin!)

'The family still farm around here, but I don't think they're bothered by goblins now. Here we are. Just drop me off here, will you? Call me any time. You know I'm happy to help you out. Bye!'

AARGH! AARGH!

(Stop it, Goblin!)

NOT FAIRY!

(Get off me! I said "sort of", which you are! Oh no! That was a clean shirt on today! Look at that! You've ruined the collar! Go away and annoy someone else!)

*****

Oooiiiooeee! Toady, Toady, Toady!

'Grmff, who's that?'

WAKEY WAKEY! ITS NEARLY MIDNIGHT, TOADY.

'Help! Who's that? I've got a gun!'

I like the nightlife. Do you like the nightlife, Toady?

'Get out!'

Uugh! The bulb must have gone, Toady, and it's oh so dark.

'Get out! Get out!'

Nice and dark for a Toady and a goblin!

'Who is this? I'm phoning the police! I've got a knife! I've got a gun! Who? Where? Nothing there. Windows? Doors? Front door? I definitely heard something, someone. I really thought it was... What was that dark stuff I was drinking in The Fox? They hadn't had that one on before. I'm gonna see them tomorrow and they'll be hearing from my lawyers! They all will!'

*****

'I was rather hoping you might learn more from the pub. There really isn't much in Metfield. I suppose there's the shop. Sue does nice cakes, if you like that sort of thing, but she won't know much about the goblin though. I still say we ought to go back to Fressingfield. Look, there's Sally!

'Slow down, Sally! You really do know how to make that little scooter move. I am impressed! I've got a friend here who wants to know about the little goblin.'

Tall! Tall!

'Actually, not little for a goblin. Quite tall for a goblin, as goblins go.'

Fifth panel!

'There, I thought you would, Sally. Sally knows all about the stories from this area. He's still being seen in his little car, but you can only see the top of his head as he whizzes past.'

Fifth panel!

(All right, Goblin!)

'No, as Sally says, he terrorised Évreux in France. You can see him on the fifth panel of Saint Taurin's reliquary.'

Tall goblin!

'And he is tall for a goblin. As I said to you earlier, he supposedly came here with Walkelin the priest during the Norman invasion. Walkelin's family have farmed here ever since, and they'll all tell you about the goblin. Originally, as Sally said, they were French, but they also appeared in parts of Germany during the Middle Ages.'

(Don't spit, Goblin!)

'I think today is the fourth Thursday, so they'll do fish and chips here in the village later. That still gives us time to... Oh dear! Look at that! That's the work of Toady Mull. I said he was a bad lot. I wonder how many of these notices he's stuck on the lamp posts. Here, read this! He's publically accused Richard Alcott of polluting the brook. He's even named him! That is bad. Poor Richard! And his poor daughter. Look there's another one, and another! Come on; let's tear these down. Don't let the bullies win, I say.

'No, he's not polluting it at all. Toady Mull's got a vendetta against him because he wants to develop a property right where Richard's workshop is. Now the young Alcott girl has got some kind of eating disorder, and we think it's all Toady's fault... No, no one can do anything about it because the parish council are so scared of him. I'll go round and see the Alcotts a bit later, but this latest development won't do Richard any good. I must say I'll be ready for a pint after all this! Then I think we should spend the evening in the pub asking about the goblin.'

*****

Oooiiieeee! Toady? Toady, Toady, Toady!

'Argh? Not again! Right, I've got a stick.'

Where's your torch, Toady? Goblin got your torch, has he?

'I'll kill you!'

Toady!

'I'll find you. I don't mind the dark.'

Goblin likes dark! Goblin likes Toady!

'I'll give you goblins! Take that! Ow! Not there! Not there!'

Goblin's got the torch! Goblin finds switch.

'You're in this cupboard, are you? Right, I'll kick the...'

TORCH!

'AARGH!!'

Goblin wants fun! Fun with Toady!

'AARGH!!'

Come back, Toady!

'Get away from me! Go on! Get away! Help! Help me!'

Come back, Toady!

'No, no, I understand. We could try the pub one more time if you like? You could have a soft drink or something? Are you sure? Because I don't mind sitting with a pint if its for your research. Fair enough. Well, I'm sorry not to have been more help. No one seems to know much about the thing these days. All we've got so far is Toady Mull accusing Mick the joiner of breaking into his house last night. He says Mick was playing at goblins, and there was a bit of a scene at Alcott's this morning. Poor Lizzie! Lizzie's the daughter. She was in the middle of it all. Most unfortunate. Mull's going mad, I think. Deluded.

'No, I don't think we should speak to them. We could pop back into Fressingfield. You know, I was thinking of trying The Fox again because it's a pity for you to have to leave without anything for your studies. If you were staying for the weekend, you could have had a pint in the village hall. They have music there on Friday nights, and everyone turns up just for the fun of it. You'd find out something there, I'm sure.

'No, I admit it's all a bit far-fetched. A goblin seen riding around in a Citroën Dyane, or rather not seen, as seems to be the case, at least lately.'

It crashed.

(It crashed? You mean you crashed it?)

'It appears he must have crashed it... No, I understand you've had enough. I hope you're not feeling too bad about coming to this place. Have a safe journey. I'll phone you if I find out any more.'

(How did you crash your car, Goblin?)

Trees!

(Perhaps you'd better stop driving.)

Toady, Toady, Toady!

'When I find out who you are, I'll kill you.'

Look, Toady. Goblin got torch again!

'Look at you! Your ugly red face!'

Look at you! Uglier redder face!

'What do you want?'

Want Toady!

'What for?'

Find treasure!

'Treasure, eh? Where is this treasure?'

Goblin knows!

'You're still breaking and entering.'

Find treasure with Toady!

'I'm still gonna find out who you are. You won't make a fool out of me.'

Toady come and find treasure!

'If this is all one big lie, you'll be hearing from my lawyers.'

*****

'I know I should have called you sooner, but better late than never... No, there's been no more goblin stories as such, but that old Citroën turned up wrecked in some woodland not far from here, and no one knows how it got there. Also, you'll be interested to know that Toady Mull was found face down in the brook. No one was at all sad about it. A few people shrugged their shoulders and said "there's a pity" and such, but I think they meant it's a pity anyone should have lived as bad a life as he did. Alcott's happier now, and his daughter's got a thing going with Mick the joiner, which is nice. The only strange thing is that if you look up the picture of the fifth frame of the Taurin reliquary, you'll see it's got two goblins on it now. I'm sure I only ever noticed one before.'

213

18. THE SECRET OF HOWLEY MARSH

As I passed the sign for Howley Marsh I suddenly felt all my sorrow and misery lift, but as soon as that sign for the slip road became diminutive in the wing mirror, it all returned.

Edith and I had rubbed along together for nearly four decades. There were no children: the gift of parenthood was never destined to be ours. We both believed in destinies, though little else, and that brought us close together, so losing her was all the more painful.

It was the time when the late snowdrops had begun to fade and the early daffodils were in full bloom. The drive to and from the hospital was the worst part. The stress of not knowing what to expect on the way there and the exquisite agony of having left her behind on the way back were akin to being forced to do something terrible against one's will. But that emotion had momentarily lifted as I passed the sign and I didn't know why.

It happened the first time a couple of weeks before her death, and then it happened again the day after that. And the next; and the next. Never in the morning, though. Driving from the west, the sign read "Marsh Howley", and as such, it had no effect on me. But coming home, it happened again and again, to the point that the knowledge that I would pass that sign would make the journey almost tolerable.

Edith died in my arms. Of course, I was desolate. I think she died about a fortnight after the phenomena had begun, but maybe it was longer. On the day of her death, I drove home almost blinded by my own tears while the wipers mopped away the relentless rain. I was already in the habit of slowing down as I passed that turn-off so as to get the most from its soothing effect. I did so on the day she died. The effect it had on me was so intensified by my grief that this time I felt as though I had been lifted bodily out of the car. Dreading the prospect of losing that relief, I thought better of driving homeward and, instead, turned off and headed for the village or, as it turned out, hamlet, that the sign had indicated would lie there.

I rolled slowly down to a T-junction, letting a lorry pass before I automatically turned left. The highway was particularly narrow at that point, so I had to back out again to allow another car to pass from the other direction. By now, the rain had stopped, so I switched off my wipers. The road soon turned into a mud track, but I drove on carefully till I was back on a solid surface.

At the entrance to the hamlet was a row of small terraced houses, seemingly deserted. As I looked across through the passenger window, I saw a woman in a flowery dress standing in a garden. Edith! My dead wife was standing in a garden in her favourite flowery dress! All wisps of doubt left me in that moment as the sight of her apparition thrilled through me like liquid fire. I jolted the car forward a few yards, made a clumsy three-point turn, and stopped by the garden. Too late, she had gone. Another woman was standing there wearing a similar dress, but I could see it wasn't Edith.

'Excuse me,' I called, rolling down the window, 'where's Edith?'

'Who?' she asked, leaning on the wall to talk to me.

'The woman who was here just a minute ago.'

'No, I didn't see any other woman.'

I wondered how she could have missed her, when it had only taken me a minute or so to turn the car around. Was this woman lying to me or was she genuinely convinced that there had been no one else?

'Are you sure?' I asked. She looked up and down the street.

'Yes,' she said, carefully regarding me. 'I came out when the rain stopped. There's been no one else.'

She had to be lying. I tried to think of something to say, but I couldn't. She turned and went back towards the house.

Edith had loved gardens. I had often seen her in our own little plot, watching her through the window of the lounge as she stood admiring a bush, or a butterfly, or some other small treasure.

I drove back to the A303 with my head spinning.

What had happened? I had felt Edith die in my arms and had lain her down on the bed, but I had most certainly just seen her in Howley Marsh. Could she have recovered? Could she then have come down here without my knowledge? I was in such a state that when I got home, I phoned the ward. They confirmed that Edith had definitely died that morning. So now I was deluded as well as bereft!

As I sorted out her effects, organised the funeral, and agonised over sending her clothes to charity shops, I felt as though I were moving through water; my senses numbed by my confused sadness.

It was a small funeral: Edith and I had kept ourselves to ourselves in latter years. That night I dreamt of Howley Marsh.

The next day, I went to the hospital to take in some flowers for the ward sister. After that, with butterflies in my guts, I was off back down the A303. As I approached the sign, the sun came out, and I saw fields of buttercups. Suddenly, I wanted to sing. Once again, I took the slip road for Howley Marsh. I hadn't got beyond the muddy track when I saw her to my left in a field. There was a small group of hikers standing by a gate, and there she was, standing in the midst of them. It was her, I know; I looked twice. I stopped the car and leapt out, slipping and slithering my clumsy feet in the mud.

'Edith! 'Edith!' I shouted and fell over onto my side.

'Take it easy, mate,' said the tallest of the hikers. 'You can't stop your vehicle here. These are all working farms. You're blocking the traffic.'

But where was Edith? She had gone. There were three women in the group all wearing the same practical trousers that she used to wear when she went out walking; but none of them were Edith.

I got up. 'Where's Edith?'

Another man spoke. 'She's not here, and you need to move.'

I stared at him. He had said, "She's not here". She's not here. That means he must know her. My heart pounded in my chest.

'Take me to Edith. Show me where she went. Tell me where she is, *please.*'

'What is he? Some kind of nut?'

A car came the other way and sounded its horn. The driver leaned out of the window and shouted, 'Oy!'

'You'd better back down the road,' said the man who knew Edith. He came towards me.

Angrily, I got back in the car. 'I will,' I said. 'I will, but I know you now, I'd recognise you again.'

'He's a nut,' said the tall man.

'Get out of the way!' yelled the driver.

The hikers moved on, and I had to reverse back all the way down the hill. Now I knew, I knew for sure. Trembling and muddy, I drove home.

The mud of Howley Marsh stuck to my clothing like glue, but I didn't wash it off. I kept touching it and feeling the warmth Edith must feel when she touches that same mud. Nor did I bathe.

The next day, I discovered the secret of the sign. There are two places. If you approach from the west, you come to the hamlet of Marsh first, so on that side of the A303, "Marsh" appears at the top of the sign. The row of terraced houses that I had discovered was in Howley. That was where I had first seen her.

This time, I took the slip road from the west. It was a longer run before I got to the muddy track, and this time I was able to drive up unimpeded. I found the terraced row and edged the car towards the garden where I had seen her on the day she died. I parked outside, got out, and waited, leaning against the wall. A few people ambled past and looked at me; curious, I think, because of the mud. So I walked up the garden path, feeling like a besotted schoolboy calling on his first crush. I rang the doorbell. No answer. I felt so sure she was near. Perhaps I should try the muddy track again. When I got back to the car, I saw how much of a mess I had made of the seat. Edith wouldn't have liked that. Still, the passenger side was clean enough. I drove on up the road and it was as I started a three-point turn that I saw her. She was in a different garden, kneeling down and scraping at something with a trowel. I switched off the engine and struggled out of the car.

'Edith!' I shouted, running towards the spot. There was a woman kneeling there doing some gardening, but it wasn't Edith. I looked all around me, to the right and to the left; she had vanished again.

'Where did she go?' I asked quickly.

'Who?'

'Edith. She was right here. You must have seen her, you absolutely must! She was wearing a grey jumper, a thick one, a bit like yours.'

'No, I don't know any Edith and certainly not here in Howley.'

'But there is one. She was here!'

'She wasn't.'

'Why won't you tell me where she is?'

Someone was standing next to my car: the tall hiker.

'You again,' he said.

'I'm looking for my wife.'

'I don't think your wife is here, and you've parked stupidly again, haven't you. You'd better stop pestering people and get out of here.'

The woman looked alarmed. 'Who is he?'

'Just someone who needs help. Now, you, go on, get on your way. And clean yourself up a bit before you scare someone else.'

'But,' I pleaded, 'I know she's here.'

'He keeps asking for Edith,' said the woman. 'And there's no Edith. I should know. I've lived here in Howley long enough.'

I scratched my head. She had been here; I would find her. There was still the field where I had seen her for the second time. They watched me get in the car.

I slowed down as I drove past the first garden, but there was still no one there. Why wouldn't anyone help me? I eased the car onto the muddy track and stopped in the arc of a passing point. Once more, I got out of the car. The beautiful mud seeped into my shoes and socks. I reached down, scooped up some of it, and took in the aroma. I rubbed it in till both hands were the colour of clay. Then I walked along the track till I came to the familiar gate where I had seen her with the hikers. I couldn't open it, so I tried to climb over, despite my arthritis. My foot got caught in the top bar, and I fell. I had a hard landing, but the pain I should have felt didn't happen. The ground was soft and smelt of childhood.

'Edith,' I whispered. 'Edith, where are you?'

I heard a comfortable buzzing noise that made me think of the two of us in our garden one summer, long ago, listening to the bees in the lavender. A tractor had stopped. Its wheels were too wide for it to get by where my car was parked.

'Are you all right?' asked the driver as he stepped down.

He opened the gate easily, and I pulled myself up onto my knees.

'Yes, yes,' I told him.

'Do you think you can drive?' he asked. 'Or shall I get help.'

'I'm looking for someone,' I said.

'Who?'

'My wife, Edith Smallwood.'

'You could try the pub. Someone's bound to know in there, but you should get cleaned up first. It's not good to ingest this stuff: it's the animals, you know.'

As I dragged myself to my feet, I scraped off some mud just to please him and squeezed into the driver's seat. I started the engine and manoeuvred further into the arc so he could get his tractor past. I smiled back when he waved in a friendly manner.

Feeling shaky, I had to drive up and down the road several times before I found the pub. The light was starting to fade and, for some reason, I parked the car at an awkward angle just inside the entrance to the car park. I couldn't seem to get the wheels aligned with the chevrons, so did what I could and just stopped. If I could find Edith here, I wouldn't drive any more. I wouldn't do anything anymore.

I was surprised to find how hard it was to get out of the car. I think I must have got chilled, causing my legs to lose their strength, and yet Edith had looked so well. Even my breath had become burdensome, and I made it to the door, puffing and panting.

The door had a delightfully traditional latch, just like the one in the house where Edith was born. Those old latches must grow stiff over the years, so I had to pull hard to get it to open. It released itself so suddenly that I stumbled inside, still holding on to it to keep me upright. There were nine or ten customers, mainly men, standing and chatting at the bar.

Their conversation ceased as I entered. I stared at them. They stared back.

'Why?' I noticed that my own voice had become raspy. What a strange day this was turning out to be. 'Why do the newly dead come to Howley Marsh?'

There was no answer.

'Tell me,' I asked. 'Why do they? Why do the newly dead come to Howley Marsh?'

Two of them approached me and I wondered why they didn't answer my question. It was when my forehead struck the floor that I realised they had come because I was falling. My thoughts dulled and my eyes failed.

Some little time later, I found myself seated at a table. A woman was bathing my face with cotton wool. I suppose some might say I had been doing the wrong thing. Every time I had seen Edith, I had taken my eyes off her. That was why she kept disappearing. I needed to have more faith, more determination. All this was so new to me: this feeling, this love.

I know I will see her again soon in Howley Marsh. And this time, when I see her, I must not take my eyes off her. I must keep my gaze fixed on her and run. I will run straight to her and let nothing get in my way. Then I will grip her so tightly that no one will ever be able to cut her loose from me. I will keep her from vanishing, and I will cry, 'Edith! Edith! Edith!'

ACKNOWLEDGEMENTS

Heather Redding, my patient first reviewer and sounding board; Sharon Perry, my brilliant proofreader and editor; Gerry and The Plough Inn; Caroline and The Bridge Inn; Kevin Smith for use of his research area, his van, and his little dog; Laura next-door; Bill Nicholson and some ex-Spurs players; and Sooty!

ABOUT THE AUTHOR

Simon J Ellis roams around a part of the country where there is literally more magic realism per square mile than anywhere else in the world. Using gossip, legend, innuendo, and unwitting fellow travellers as his source, he has suffused these stories with more truth than is probably legal.

He has hit upon a unique writing method that involves getting up late in the day, eating plenty of avocados, and avoiding work at all costs. He spends his time searching for outrageous anecdotes, which he then throws at his muse when she is at her most hung over.

The work ethic, being the antithesis of the creative soul, has had no part to play in the production of this slender volume; rather it has come about simply by sitting in pubs and absorbing all sorts of specialist nonsense. The bits that seem the most unlikely are probably the bits that are true.

THE LEA BRIDGE ROAD SHANTY MEN

What is the connection between a man attacked at night on the Lea Bridge Road and a young girl tracked and lured by rival gangs? In this fast-moving narrative, a group of East London schoolgirls, honing their act as shanty singers, end up embarking on a roller coaster ride from East London to Bristol, Devon, and Cornwall. At the same time, recently-released convict, Marcus Okeke, is trying to make contact with his estranged daughter, but in order to understand the forces that are keeping them apart, he must first confront his own dark past.

FRANCIS TROCKLEY REGGAE MAN

Francis Trockley, a neglected white boy, finds an outlet for his self-expression in Rastafari. His odyssey begins during a football match when his school burns down. Catapulted into a new life with a different circle of friends, he quickly finds himself in love and follows a path that leads him into some very dark places. In his downward spiral, he becomes the catalyst for something that happened before he was born. What began with blood must end with blood.

THE BEAUFORT STIPENDIARY

The good Christians in the village of Aldstone have finally renovated the church, but the bishop is unable to justify a full-time vicar. Wealthy Jock Beaufort steps in and foots the bill, but his dealings with a number of pharmaceutical firms does not sit well with the new incumbent's views on morality. As he wrestles with his conscience, his daughter decides to take matters into her own hands, and the ensuing story of love and betrayal transcends not only their little world, but also the bigger world around them.

Printed in Great Britain
by Amazon